GW01453007

FOX GOLD

FOX GOLD

NIGHTINGALE ISLAND

BOWL OF ROSES

by

George Moor

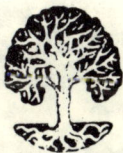

JOHN CALDER
LONDON

First published in Great Britain 1978
by John Calder (Publishers) Ltd
18 Brewer Street, London W1R 4AS

ISBN 0 7145 3615 6 casebound

Type set in 11pt Baskerville by Woolaston Parker Ltd. Leicester

Printed in Scotland by M&A Thomson Litho Ltd. East Kilbride
and bound by Hunter & Foulis Ltd. Edinburgh

CONTENTS

Fox Gold

PRELUDE

Sam Ryder, known as Young Sam, despite his sixty-five years, to distinguish him from his long-dead father, came quietly through the woods. The fallen beech leaves of this year as well as all the years before, acted as a rug to his feet in their clogs without irons.

He had crossed Crush Water by the iron and concrete fisherman's bridge (brooding as he did so on the iniquities of the Hugley Angling Club whose lease of the water he would not renew) and taken the barely noticed track, little more than a sunken line of damp fallen leaves, which climbed diagonally from the valley floor to the clear view of Little Height.

Few excursionists came this way, even at weekends, and if they did they were disappointed, for the way ended in a precipice and they were forced to turn back. Still, their journey had terminated in the exhilarating prospect of Fox Hollow and the sea-like breeziness of the moors, and it cost them nothing.

Uphill and on the flat Young Sam moved neither slowly nor swiftly, but with steady ungainliness. He was a small stocky figure in a rather grubby mackintosh with an ill-rolled umbrella under one arm; he did not use the umbrella as an aid-stick as this helped to wear out ferrules and ferrules cost brass.

Possibly at such an early hour nobody's face could have radiated much sweetness, but Sam's face was singularly unexpressive; it was as welcoming as a washing-board, and as raw and lined. It had the grittiness of the millstone grit under the turf on which he was walking. He was not one given to flashy exhibitions of feeling or tenderness of mood. From his face no one would have guessed, though, that his sentiments were at their most agreeable as he came on to the level dew-dainty turf and heather avenue which led between young birches, like the lined approach to a shrine in its sacred grove, to the view over Fox Hollow.

This natural avenue near Little Height was a curious and haunting place, and was indeed not natural. In 1904 a reservoir had been constructed in the heart of the moors and a temporary one-line railway for the transport of materials had been constructed from Hugley to the work-site. This railway had swung into the valley from near Buver Holes. Near Little Height at that time there had been nothing except a great natural quarry, a cliff face of boulders and chasmed outcrops of rock then forming one side of Fox Hollow.

An embankment, dyke-like in shape, had been built to support the railway lines, and it was along this former railway track, returned to nature for almost fifty years, that Young Sam was now walking.

To the left was a descent into the bouldered and chaotic rock hollow of the former natural quarry which had been there before the railway came; on the right was a thickly wooded drop into the valley with on the other side of the Water, the unoccupied small-paned game-keeper's cottage of Underwood just visible and somewhat insubstantial in the unwinding morning mists.

Of the raw exposure of rock fifty years ago there was no trace. Nature had healed back; but with a newness of perfection found nowhere else in Crush Valley. Instead of sphagnum moss and coarse sword-grass there was tender turf, nurtured by the equable mixture of sunshine and showers in this valley-corner, and heather, not wiry like blackened mattress springs, but of delicate dark young green and exquisitely stitched sprays of white-pink and purple. The bilberries here in early summer were of a luscious fulness like garden grown blackcurrants.

It was beautiful here at noon when the young birches provided pennants of shade, or near sunset when all of Fox Hollow lay hushed in heather-withering peace and a great red ball of sun tinged the moors and moor-waters crimson. But in the first mists of morning, the sun not yet above the hills, the valley seemed to lurk. The infinitely languid mists were like lazy assassins—a tall figure would, almost mockingly, vanish into the trees, or a genii would grow up tall from the turf. What came close did not touch, nor could the human eye distinguish when nothingness became nothing.

There was a surge and mockery of elegant ghosts.

Pagodas trembled among the pines. Who in a loose summer gown slipped inside?

Yet there was nothing, except cunning illusion.

The very objects one recognized were no longer the same: this rock, this great-rooted tree, seen isolated, became monstrous, enchanted and creatured in themselves.

Young Sam was reminded of the two Chinese wall-scrolls hanging in the gallery at home, the little male figure in them dwarfed by waterfalls and mist-wound hills.

Usually on his early morning strolls Young Sam would bring one of the hounds with him. Perhaps it was the absence of a panting noisily eager companion straining on the leash that made him today feel so strongly the sneaking quiet in the mist. He who did so much watching of others had a sense now not so much of being watched as surrounded.

He stopped, and he saw it.

Jutted from the platform of Little Height was the substantial wraith, the grey presence with the sharp silhouetted ears. Seemingly the beast was not aware of Young Sam's approach as it surveyed with easy lordship the territory that was Young Sam's property. But with easy familiarity it dominated not only the land but the sky against which it stood. It looked as if it had alit. It looked as if it was not.

But it was, for its head turned. Immediately it was tensed, and with a sardonic, ineffably cool and sardonic grin, it vanished. Not a leaf stirred. It had melted into mist, disappeared into earth and trees.

Young Sam brought up his hand and with his knuckles rubbed his eyes.

There was nothing so extraordinary in seeing a fox here, he told himself, though this one had affected him as if he had seen a wolf. The mist had contributed an illusion of size, increasing the impression of power. But there had been a daintiness, a trimness, about the figure. He would have sworn it was grey, woven of mist, though he knew from other foxes, mainly dead, that he had seen, there must be reds and browns in its coat.

What shocked and left him shaken with a disagreeable disquiet like nausea, was the thing's superiority. He had seen it so clearly like a giant gryphon surveying its territory, 'my land', Ryder land, with such an air of undoubted possession and mastery. Then, worst of all, it had given the real owner and legal master a look of such utter sneezing contempt that Young Sam felt the look had passed into and weakened his bones.

Now he no longer knew whether he had seen or whether he had imagined, but the fox-face, or fox-mask, in its sneering immobility, had it not a shrunken sardonic expression like the Devil's?

Could he have seen the Devil?

Or the bacon he'd had for breakfast that morning, the cheaper cut from Warburton's Stores, could it be giving him hallucinations like mushroom poisoning?

There was nothing so extraordinary in seeing a fox some-where so near Fox Hollow. He'd heard no complaints from his tenant farmers about any foxes recently raiding their poultry. With the rabbits reduced one might have expected it. The few rabbits left in the valley nowadays looked like hares. If the fox he had just seen were living on them, no wonder it too, looked bigger!

He walked towards the place where the fox had vanished. It probably had its earth somewhere near. There were no open-ings in the ground on top of the old embankment, but in the natural quarry behind there were fissures, crevices and small caves galore. These went back and down into the main hillside. If the fox were there, Young Sam thought with a recoil of distaste as he remembered the sneering mask, it would be virtually living under the foundations of his house, The Lees, far deep down beyond the reach of his hounds, sneering at him. . . .

A little further on the path ran along the side of a wall. By a gate he entered a field at the back of The Lees.

He would have a word with Warburton about that bacon. It had tasted proper reesty. For one pound a pound you didn't have to accept something the bluebottles had walked over or get food poisoning, even if you did not expect the best quality ham either. It had felt quite peculiar for a moment, imagining an everyday ordinary little fox to be the Devil.

CHAPTER ONE

The great iron gate of The Lees creaked open. Dusk was beginning but Young Sam had not yet lit the green lamp.

Now at the gate's creaking the hounds immediately began yelling and the electric lights came on inside and outside the solarium and glass-walled extension that he liked to use as a lounge. His small face ballooned behind the glass, ascertaining who had opened the gate.

A woman was fumbling to sneck back the great weight of the gate which fell inward. A driveway of stone-setts led to the house and the tithe-barn with its immense dilapidating roof of heavy thatch-stones.

The hounds became abruptly silent. Young Sam, commanding them into the main structure of the old hall, was waiting for his mysterious visitor to explain herself. Visitors to The Lees were always rare; unauthorized ones unheard of.

If she were coming to collect for charity, she must be from outside the parish. She wore sensible shoes that scraped and echoed on the setts. Her suit was brown, and her face looked very white. A town dweller he supposed. Quite a well-built piece of womanhood, he appraised, for though a bachelor of sixty-five Young Sam had developed to a high pitch his sense of valuation—whether of property or livestock or food. He would put her around thirty-five to thirty-eight. With approval he marked that she did not use make-up. An assurance about her led him to guess that she was either a nurse or a widow, habitual intercourse with bed-pans in one case and male quirks in the other having rubbed off any virgin shyness. Not bold, he summed up, but no violet.

Then (as he felt a little flustered) she was pressing the bell.

He was completely unshaven as (razor-blades costing money) he shaved only on those days when he had business and outside contact with the world. He was wearing moreover, a striped collarless flannel shirt that came from some stock made in 1899 and never sold. His trousers were doubly supported by a big pair of grey braces and a big leather belt that had survived from his 1918 uniform. He had not asked the wench to call. Still, he would have liked to look a bit more groomed.

'Mr Ryder?' she smiled, all little pearl teeth, with womanly scent deliciously gassing him.

'I am,' he boomed.

'Oh I'm so sorry to be troubling you at this hour, but I was wondering if I could have a word with you about possibly taking over the tenancy of Underwood.'

'You're not from these parts,' Young Sam stated rather than accused.

'I'm from Manchester,' she responded.

His backbone stiffened. 'I'll not have any weekenders. We'll have nowt of that sort. I had a couple once from Salford and, by gum, they did a midnight flitting and took the lavatory seat. It was a good-grained ashwood,' he growled throatily, 'and by present reckoning it would fetch some good money. I'll have no weekending trash from places like yon.'

'Oh but Mr. Ryder,' she cried girlishly with an endearing feminine gurgle, 'I want it for permanent occupation. I wouldn't dream of troubling you about taking it just for weekends.'

'Would you keep a good fire going?'

'Most certainly—I would make my own bread.'

Young Sam stood, somewhat troubled by the recollection of the lavatory seat. He had been seldom bested but he had a prodigious memory for the rare occasions when he had been outsmarted by villainous human nature. He motioned her inside.

'And you don't get them made like that any more now,' he complained nostalgically. 'Not with the two holes. Back to backs we called 'em.'

The visitor smiled mysteriously. Perhaps she was not certain whether he were referring to bread baking or lavatory seats. But as—the first female in two years—she came over the threshold of The Lees, there was this smile on her lips and in her eyes. Her hair was auburn—not from a bottle, he supposed, but there was no telling with female creatures nowadays—and her eyes, if brown, had a considerable element of gold or red. He did not want to stare directly into her eyes but they seemed to run or dance with the golden-red—or would yellow be more accurate? He was somewhat disconcerted.

'So you're thinking of living at Underwood?' he remarked, not to let her feel self-conscious at his furtive side-glance at her unusual eyes. 'There's no goodness in this modern shop-made bread.'

The dogs were growling restlessly on the other side of the door.

'Shut your yap,' he bawled.

'I like a nice home-made cob,' she said demurely.

'Ah,' he sighed. 'It was a good baking-oven at Underwood in Tom Lumb's time. His missus made a famous nettle-beer too. None of this fizzy modern muck,' he said fiercely. Then: 'Would you like a spot of whisky? You need summat to keep these nasty Autumn mists off the chest.'

'It's very kind of you,' she laughed, and as this was plainly no refusal he took it for consent. The bottle and glasses were conveniently near.

'To your good health,' she said, sipping.

'To yours,' he said with a grim smile. He swallowed, asked abruptly: 'What makes you want to leave Manchester?'

'I manage a grocery shop,' she said. 'Now it's closing. The supermarkets are taking business from the old grocery chain-stores, though the same people own both, I believe.'

'I haven't asked your name yet, you know,' he said gruffly.

'Oh. Mrs. Fox.'

'What about Mr. Fox?'

'He was fatally injured,' she said slowly, 'in an industrial accident.' She seemed to be smiling with the same strange smile with which she had come into The Lees. Young Sam was surprised, but the smile, he supposed, rose from nervousness. Her eyes *were* gold, like the whisky.

'It's eight pounds a week,' said Young Sam, 'and the tenant pays rates. There's good running water—none better in the Riding—and no electricity. You'll not be liable to get any shocks that way. One more thing—I look after the roof and gutters, but you undertake the inside decorations and the outside painting which must be white. I'll have no filthy gaudy muck on my premises. If you like duck-egg blue round your windows better go and live at Blackpool!'

She nodded. He refilled her glass and his own.

'I've been offered all sorts of money for the place,' he volunteered, 'but I want none of them weekenders. A regular tenant who keeps the place warmed—and doesn't go in for sub-letting—is what I prefer. Otherwise it will stand empty. The Lumbs lived there till five years after the war. You can't get skilled repair-men who'll live so far out nowadays. These modern people can't live without their cinemas and electricity and television. Even the children expect to be taken to school in a taxi. They'd do better staying at home, most of 'em, I reckon. There's a nice pig-sty at Underwood—you could get a couple of gilts and keep a goat in the barn. Tom Lumb was fond of bantams, but a few proper sized hens would be more to the purpose, I reckon.'

'I would like some hens,' spoke Mrs. Fox dreamily.

The whisky had warmed Young Sam's stomach and now he saw his visitor in golden fire, the reddish hair and white face wavering clouded, the lips smiling with little red hairs shining at each side of the mouth. He pulled out his big red and white spotted handkerchief and dabbed his brow.

'I'll just put the dogs in,' he said, 'and fetch you a rent-book and the key.'

He roared the bloodhounds down into their quarters in the cellar and returning, looked for a rent-book in the study. While he was about it, he lit the hanging oil-lamp with the green shade. Though the house was extensively wired for electricity, when by himself he kept to paraffin as more economical and pleasant. It was an absolute disgrace to a civilized county that the electricity bills each quarter were so high and liable to errors. He kept a strict watch on The Lees' meters.

Now this woman . . . Penny rent-book and key in hand, he stood and pondered. There was something odd about her. She had reddish hair like his mother. It was the eyes that were odd —un-English. Of course coming from Manchester she might have a touch of the Irish. She had no wedding ring on her finger. It would have been better to have seen her widow's pension book, but presumably she would be able to pay. . . .

'Of course you realize it's not what you would call furnished,' he said stepping back into the room.

'Not furnished? That of course is the problem, how to get my furniture there. My beautiful new standard-lamp will be no use at all.'

'There's a table of sorts and a few chairs. Enough to get by on, apart from bedding.'

'And no bed?'

'There's a cupboard bed downstairs—and you'll find it right useful in the winter when you can sleep down where the fire is. They're very useful in the cold weather, those old panelled beds. There may be an old mattress on it, left by the last fellow who had the place, a bird-watcher. Of course it would need airing. Aye, he was a right funny fellow, that,' said Young Sam reflectively. 'I told him to take an umbrella with him, but he said he didn't think them manly. They're a sight more sensible than getting drenched to the hide, I told him. But he went his own road and it was no surprise to me when he got pneumonia. Some things you don't economize on,' said Young Sam firmly, 'not in the end.'

He had been writing in the rent-book in his sloping and angular old-fashioned handwriting. 'Mrs. . . . what are your initials?'

'P—for Peggy,' said Mrs. Fox.

'You mean M—for Margaret,' declared Young Sam.

'No, I'm a Peggy. I was registered as Peggy.'

'But you can't be christened Peggy. It's got to be Margaret.'

'I was never christened,' said Mrs. Fox smiling. Young Sam dropped the pen in his astonishment.

'Never christened? Why, then th'art nobbut a heathen! Eeah!'

He was so shocked that he had to pour himself a whisky to compose himself.

'No, not for me,' said the unbaptized creature. 'I've got to see my way back tonight—I should explain that I was born overseas where there were no facilities for baptism. I should think my father had enough trouble getting me even registered and he naturally put on the form the name by which they knew me. Nobody objected.'

'You could have had it done to you later,' said Young Sam recovering.

'I've never felt any different,' said Mrs. Fox.

'Tha might have felt no different. But the's different from every other chrissom soul. Why,' said Young Sam and he could have spoken with no more impressive seriousness if he had discovered a flaw in her investments, 'tha has done theeself out of all chance of salvation. Damned everlasting—that's what tha'll be. I reckon most of 'em all go that road. But tha's *certain*. You come to the stoup at Rossall Church and I'll be your god-father.'

'I'll think of it,' said Mrs. Fox with her nervous smile.

'Thinking draws no water from the well. You want to get cracking. It takes no more than two–three minutes and then tha stands some chance. I'd not be done out of my Salvation for the lack of a few drops of water,' said Young Sam stoutly.

'Maybe I shall then,' said Mrs. Fox. 'You are very eloquent, Mr. Ryder. But you know, I'm a bit worried about my bus.'

Young Sam fished out his turnip watch of dulled silver. 'The one from Buver Holes is on the hour. You'll have to catch the next; you've missed this. There's no sense in waiting in the cold up there. Let me show you the house.'

'I'd be delighted.' Mrs. Fox smoothed down her skirt as they arose.

He set on the master-switch so that in an instant the house inside and outside poured brilliance. When the occasion demanded, Young Sam could be munificent, even with electricity, and now was such an occasion. The lawns were all lit from lights set in the branches of the old trees. From the road the old stone of the house would be seen floodlit from the peaked seventeenth century gables with their surmounted stone balls.

Before her Mrs. Fox saw beautifully polished wood-floors, and the electric polisher which Young Sam had not had the time or strength to put away. He hastened into the study to turn out the paraffin lamp which was burning wastefully.

'There's nowt much there,' he said shutting the study door

and turning her towards the hall and what was in fact the true entrance to the house though he made no use of it.

It was unlikely that Mrs. Fox was aware of the signal courtesy being extended to her. Young Sam drove back all cultural organizations and groups (mainly of female membership) that by post and phone endeavoured to intrude into the treasure-packed privacy of his bachelor homestead. The National Trust had given a nasty lead in this direction, he felt, not to speak of those benighted nobles who made a zoo of themselves for ten pence. As for individuals—'I don't come wanting to go walking through your house, do I?' he would snap at some poor fellow from Brighouse. 'Looking at your pots and pans and the state of your sink. Stay in your own home and I'll stay in mine.' When antiquaries from York arrived unheralded to view the great tithe-barn, he had simply turned the dogs loose. Gawping through other's windows was all some folk had a mind to nowadays.

The Ryders were not an old family and had been at The Lees only since the seventeenth century, but they had been wealthy there right through the eighteenth century. As they were a family that saved and hoarded everything, and never broke anything, they had passed on to Young Sam, the last of the line, one of the finest repositories of living eighteenth century antiques not yet on the way to New York. Young Sam was aware of the value of the gold, the silver and silver-gilt collections, but he scarcely regarded the grandfather and Dresden clocks or the china pieces under glass in the light of antiques. They were just the furniture of his home.

Mrs. Fox seemed to be struggling to find some appropriate utterance as she found herself beleaguered in thickets of Chinese screens, eighteenth century ormolu-inlaid tables supporting elaborate clocks of Dresden statuettes in glass cases.

'Mind the flex,' Young Sam would say as they would come up against yet another vacuum cleaner lying where he had left it. 'It's a never-ending battle with dust.'

There was no dust, though, to be seen anywhere—a testimony to his diligence. 'This doll's house was made by Chippendale, so they say. A proper dust-trap,' he pronounced with disgust.

'Do you mean to say, Mr. Ryder, that you do all this

cleaning by yourself?'

'Who else?' he asked with surprise. 'This is the woollen area and you won't find women coming cleaning when they can earn twice as much in the mills. My housekeeper retired three years ago when she was eighty. I did have someone in,' he said recollecting Mrs. Hoyle, the wife of his agent, 'but she was a real dying duck. Nothing but cups of tea and gab, gab, gab, so I've made to shift for myself.' They were now ascending the stairs, haunted by old glooming clocks that also told you the phase of the moon. 'The old country woman who could do a week's baking and see to the pigs and hens is dying. They paint their faces like whores and live out of tins. They're no more use on a farm than yon china doll. There's hardly any on 'em now that will wear clogs—all their thought's on getting to a dance on Saturday neet.'

'Why, what's this?' his visitor exclaimed.

He peered. 'Oh, those—there's two of them. They're foxes. They come from a shrine in Japan or China—they're sort of gods there. Heathen, you know. Most of the stuff up here came from my mother's family. That's her portrait there. It was painted before I was born,' he said with noticeable tenderness, turning from the two images of the foxes perched upright with their tails standing in comic formality straight against their backs, and switching on two barred lights that softly illumined the portrait from above and below.

The portrait, by some provincial Whistler and less impressive than the few smoky old oils of dark grim earlier Ryders, showed a woman in a white dress. She was in her late thirties—Young Sam had been the only child of old parents. Her hair was a light red-brown, and her hands were peacefully folded. She was smiling, but her eyes looked sad.

'Her hair is the same as yours,' spoke Young Sam.

'Your mother?' Mrs. Fox asked.

'Yes, my mother.' With a sigh he switched off the lights, and they descended the stairs.

Among the china-cabinets, the inlaid tables and Dresden clocks again, he remarked, 'Tha might as well see the wash-cellar.' This was down a flight of stone-stairs and the excited yelling of the dogs sounded close. 'Don't worry. They're in another part,' said Young Sam seeing the sudden tension in Mrs. Fox's face.

She came, surprised, into the brightness of what he had called the wash-cellar. There was a de-luxe washing machine, a spin-dryer and drying cabinets. The gleaming spotless enamel and the twentieth century machines and appliances were unexpected after the jumble of earlier centuries upstairs.

In the next cellar were the refrigerators. From there they came up into the kitchen which was unexpectedly equipped with modern labour-saving devices. Next to the electric cooker was the primus burner which Young Sam preferred to use as more reliable and economical.

'You've everything,' Mrs. Fox commented.

'So to speak,' said Young Sam somewhat dolefully. All the modern devices and appliances, including the Rolls Royce which with the other car were stabled nowadays in unused museum spotlessness in the great tithe-barn, had been obtained from no inclination of his own but to bring comfort and convenience to the two inescapably ageing women who had watched over him. . . . He lowered his head, as if consulting his watch. 'Well, you'll make it easily,' he said more briskly. 'There's plenty of lights all along the road so you're not likely to get wandering lost. Can you pay a month in advance for the tenancy, starting this Saturday? And there'll be a pound too for the lamp—it hangs from the beam.'

Mrs. Fox produced several five pound notes from her purse. Young Sam entered the sum in the rent-book, signing with his angular 'S.R.' gave her change of some pound notes and small change from a saucer, and presented it to her.

'I'm so pleased at the thought of living at Underwood,' said Mrs. Fox.

'The postman won't be if he has to take letters there every day,' Young Sam commented in grim amusement. 'The track there takes a Land-Rover, but it would be no good for a pantechnicon. You'd be advised to get Bancrofts at Hugeley to transfer your furniture on to one of their vehicles.'

'Thank you for all your help,' said Mrs. Fox, 'and for showing me your most interesting house.'

'It's been a rare pleasure,' spoke Young Sam standing a small scruffy figure in the lighted doorway as Mrs. Fox departed over the setts towards the iron gate. He spoke the truth—a strange female visiting The Lees was indeed a rarity. By tomorrow the news would be spreading all over the parish. He had heard the whine of a bicycle passing along the road and whoever it was had observed Mrs. Fox's departure and all the lights on at The Lees.

Stepping back in, Young Sam turned the switch to 'off' and The Lees was no longer in an expanse of light. He picked up the notes to take to the study but before going there descended to let out the dogs. With them about The Lees was safe from prowlers.

CHAPTER TWO

Once, at an official county reception in the days when he still attended such things, Young Sam had been lightly interrogated by the wife of a county alderman, 'But what do you do to pass the days, Mr. Ryder?'

Young Sam, confronted with this classic example of Bradford's town cultured inanity for what do people anywhere do if they have money, had crushingly and not quite truthfully retorted, 'I read the Good Book, ma'am!'

It was the only book he did read—a chapter a day. He preferred the Old Testament as being in general more true to life, and he liked the beginning and the ending best. Genesis seemed to him credible; looking over the Pennine hills he could just imagine God setting about it in that way. Revelations similarly gave a convincing outline of how the earth would soon be ending. He could not truthfully say that he cared much for the fanciful parts of the New Testament. He thought it very improbable that Christ would have insulted the backbone of any congregation as he was represented as doing in the parable of Dives and Lazarus, and there were obvious omissions in the text such as the recommendation to restore the birch which some sentimental Apostle had surreptitiously obliterated. He would have no radio at The Lees; the weather reports he considered as meddling with God's business, and full of London bias. He had not looked at The Yorkshire Post since Mrs. Horsfall the old housekeeper, had retired; he considered that it encouraged frivolity and modern art.

No, he read the letters about his investments and a chapter of the Bible, and while the daylight lasted he had his telescope. It was of the best German manufacture, and was set up in a small eighteenth century arbour connected by a covered way to the house. The telescope was famous in the parish and much respected by Young Sam's tenant farmers. By its aid he missed nothing. From his commanding position behind The Lees he could train it on all his property. He knew which farmer had deliberately brought a myxomatosis-infected rabbit into the woods to get rid of the disease-free rabbits there. He had acquired more lore about the country habits of young couples than any other in a parish given to intense interest in such matters. In fact awareness of Young Sam's telescope tended to keep young couples out of the woods.

When he had encountered angry remonstrance, Young Sam made no secret of his watching and declared, 'If they weren't doing something they were ashamed of, they'd have nowt to say.'

His nosiness was of a patriarchal directness and innocence. 'Was that your Meggy I saw cleaning your windows this forenoon?' he would enquire of Mrs. Shaw whose farm lay some miles off on top of Corbett Knoll. 'I couldn't right make out with just t'arm showing.' Or Mrs. Jump who had a small-holding in the direction of Buvers Hole would be greeted with, 'That were a wopping big gooseberry on t'bush under t'window, but it would have been sweeter with yan more day's sunning.' However, as in the centre of the Pennines a piped sewerage system is not a practicable proposition and people must make do with wooden earth-closets standing upright like coffins and with doors that frequently spring open in the brisk winds, it cannot be denied that Young Sam's telescope was resented as betraying human dignity.

Old Sam, who had owned most of the mills in Hugeley, insisted on his workers attending either church or chapel on Sunday mornings and up to the Great War resisted the stirrings of the unions, had been a hated man, though he had no telescope. Young Sam, who had inherited the considerable fortune and property of his mother's family the Corbetts as well as his father's entire estate, was hated both for this and for his telescope. His father's reputation for harshness descended to him, though in point of fact Young Sam had long retired from all active involvement in the mills, and his interest in the farms, if too close for comfort, was always scrupulously just. He laid out more in the upkeep and proper maintenance of his property than he in fact received.

The telescope was resented as evidence of the feudal domi-
nance of his wealth and his furtive sexual interests. His was
certainly not the only telescope in active use in far-flung
Rossall Parish. But his was indisputedly the most expensive and
efficient. He could give it full-time attention for he had no need
to break off for work or to collect his pension.

Thus, on the Saturday, he saw one of Bancroft's small
waggons piled with furniture creeping along the path to
Underwood. Mrs. Fox in an aster-coloured dress was seated
beside the driver. He saw her clambering out and noticed what
a superb figure she had. He could see her pearly teeth in a smile
as she strove with the large key to open the stiff door of Underwood. Her red hair stood out against the faded white paintwork
as she wrestled with the lock.

'Firm—lift up—relax, then turn,' I should have told her,'
Young Sam murmured. The driver came to help her but had
no success. At last, by herself when about to give up, she found
the right way.

Young Sam watched what was taken in—a little three-piece
suite of dark green, bedding, a pink laundry-basket. . . . A
column of smoke showed that the fire had been lit. When the
waggon was empty, the driver disappeared into the cottage.

'Having a cup of tea,' Young Sam told himself.

It was a lengthy cup of tea, though, and no mistake (thought
Young Sam)' but then perhaps she could not get the primus
going or was even boiling the water on the fire. It was approaching dusk when the driver finally came out, reversed his vehicle
near the pig-sty and drove back through the woods.

Mrs. Fox continued settling in. Dusk hampered precise
observation but he could see her moving downstairs in the
fire's glow and upstairs amid a bobbing of candles. Finally she
lit the downstairs lamp.

She came out a few times and threw things on the garden.
One object he identified as the old mattress which had been in
the cupboard bed.

'Throwing away good flock!' he muttered. 'She could have
shifted the lot into a clean sugar-bag.'

At seven o'clock the garden burst into flame. The pale
outside of the cottage was washed with red-gold, and spangling

gold stars rushed with the wind into the woods.

'Mercy on us—she'll burn the district down,' thought Young Sam, horrified, comprehending that she had made a bonfire of all the old gear in the cottage, with paraffin poured on.

He could see her, exultant-faced, the skin glowing golden red from the blaze. The pins had come out of her hair which streamed like a Communist banner or a fox's brush in the night-breeze.

'It's not right,' Young Sam thought, appalled by the suggestions of female violence within the range of his telescope, 'standing there with next to nowt on and I dare say with not a penny's insurance. Paraffin-crazy! That were a good forty pennorth she must have poured on! And it's not even Bonfire Neet!'

Though he waited, he was not given the opportunity of calling the Hugeley fire-brigade and finding out if they were at such a pitch of preparedness as their portion of the rates demanded. The bonfire collapsed to a little red point and died.

Mrs. Fox's lamp was still on, wasting oil, when Young Sam himself was ready for bed. As he donned his night-shirt, he had uneasy forebodings that in Mrs. Fox—unchristened to boot—there might lurk strange fires, whole dry kegs of combustible nature. . . . He must remember to buy her a bin so she would have no excuse to burn everything.

On Sunday, when Young Sam attended both the morning and evening services at Rossall Parish Church, Mrs. Fox seemed to spend the best part of the day in bed. He wondered if she was reading the Good Book from the mattress, but thought it unlikely. But being at Underwood did prevent her reading the evil newspapers which darkened England every Sunday. Whatever Magna Carta or the Civil War, or the Gettysburg Address implied, Young Sam was not going to have his tenants reading wicked filthy trash on the Lord's Day, and that was final. As a result no newspapers were delivered to tenants of his property on Sunday, but the farmers who lived far out duly collected their Sunday newspapers from Hugeley on Monday.

Mrs. Fox had lit a fire by five o'clock and after drinking a lot of coffee she cooked a couple of chops for herself, Young

Sam was able to ascertain before he was obliged to depart for Evening-Song.

Monday brought the dust-cart to The Lees. It was scheduled to arrive around two o'clock but Young Sam liked to get up especially early on Mondays and polish and prime the guns.

The Ten Commandments say 'Thou shalt not kill' but they also say 'Thou shalt not steal.' In any case Young Sam would fire without any intention to kill; he would hope just to maim. In these times when the birch is not used on the deserving—such as Moggy Greenwood—and the police have gone soft, a man must stand up for his own rights.

Greenwood Quintus Greenwood, Moggy's father, had never bought a dog or radio license in his life, and he had once been fined seven and sixpence at the Magistrate's Court for breaking Dora Midgeley's clothes-prop and calling her a 'meddlesome owld bitch'. It was only to be expected that the son of such a father would appear in the Juvenile Court at Pilney on his eighth birthday for stealing the infant school's milk-money from his form-mistress Miss Lemon. Several appearances later he was brought up in court by his own father for robbing the gas-meter, but the charge was dismissed after Moggy accused the old man of taking the money himself and framing him. He was put on probation for taking a motor cycle without the owner's permission and driving without lights. While on probation he was accused of attempted rape and put in a Rehabilitation Centre. Emerging bronzed, he vanished from Hugeley into the Royal Navy. He was ordered to be dismissed from the service after confinement for a rainbow of charges including tormenting the ship's cat, Sodomy and selling the ship's entire stock of candles and ox-tail soup, to a Tamil in Singapore. Moggy claimed that he had got next to nothing from the transaction.

Back in Hugeley, Moggy (who had acquired the nickname by then) married Deirdre Midgeley, from next door, as if to prove his normality. Eight months later the battle of the separation orders began, Moggy claiming, when up in court for robbing the till and stealing four bottles of stout from the Buvers Hole Working-Men's Club, that he had been desperate for money to clothe and feed his wife and young baby. He was bound over. But for the series of burglaries in Dawson Street during the Wakes Week he was sentenced to twelve months. As during Wakes Week nobody in Dawson Street had any money to leave behind, Moggy had acquired mounds of fruit-dishes from the sideboards for which he got next to nothing from the woman who kept the second-hand stall in Pilney Market. Major Monckton in sentencing Moggy had severely declared, 'You have got to learn before it is too late that crime just does not pay.'

At a pleasantly old-world red-brick prison in the Midlands (Wakefield being full up), Moggy had soon become a trusty and was put in charge of towels for the prisoners' weekly baths. He emerged pale and fat, vowing that he would kill himself rather than endure the stinking jug again. A Free Church minister took an interest in his case and since nobody else would employ him in Hugeley (his brief time on a coal-cart had ended after complaints from housewives of getting lighter hundredweights) he had been steered into employ at the crematorium. He was caught red-handed on the Old Scots Road wheeling a coffin on his bicycle; he claimed he was taking it home to make a rabbit-hutch. As the manager admitted he had said Moggy could take the old wood at the back of the building, no charges were brought. The indefatigible minister found Moggy a position as spare grave-digger. Moggy, after one grave, discovered a weakness in his back and went on sickness benefit and the dole. He lived on fish and chips, paid no maintenance for the children (claiming the twins were not his) and drank copiously at The Pale Apprentice with Billy O'Neill and the local roaring boys. Moggy and O'Neill were handed down sentences of two years each, while the other four got off more lightly, for their part in blasting a safe from the biggest mill in the district. They had blown the wall down with the safe landing unharmed in the river. They were engaged in salvage operations when arrested, and learnt later that there was nothing in the safe except new patterns.

In the course of evidence given by plain-clothes detectives who had spent many evenings at The Pale Apprentice, Young Sam's name, to his indignation, had come into this notorious case. O'Neill and Moggy had at first envisaged breaknig into

The Lees. From remarks made by the gang it appeared that they considered The Lees to be stocked from cellars to attic with gold. 'Th'owld boy sits trickling guinea-pieces through his fingers by light of a paraffin lamp,' O'Neill had said. 'He's been seen. He won't spend owt but lives on oxo-cubes which he whips from Woolworth's.'

'He's a cunning old basket,' Moggy was reported as saying. 'Old Sam had my grandad turned off from work. Happen we'd have to put him to sleep.'

It was this difficulty of disposing of Young Sam and risking their valuable necks for hitting him too hard that finally turned the pub-gang to the simpler task of entering and robbing the mill. Young Sam had been furious at the oxo-cube innuendo and immediately had the latest burglar-alarms and devices installed at The Lees. He had also acquired the dogs.

Young Sam remembered how angry his father had been at Brutus Cassius Greenwood, a revolutionary wretch descended from a long line of trouble-makers related to the bloodthirsty ruffian who had knocked off Good King Charles' block, and so it was not an utter surprise to him that his own assassination had been contemplated by Moggy of that black line. He had been indignant at Moggy's getting away with a mere two-years when he would have willingly worked a gibbet or gallows for anyone who had even thought about stealing his belongings.

If Moggy had been birched in youth, lashed to the mast, keelhauled and manacled in the navy, knouted to dig quarries with his teeth by prison-warders and sent regularly to Sunday school, he would be a law-abiding post-office assistant or an inoffensive insurance-agent. O'Neill being Irish and a Papist naturally knew no better, and in any case he was back in prison for selling cold tea as the best Scottish whisky at Christmas time. But Moggy, the product of modern English sentimental softness and the sort of unholy blackguard who would mow down the Czar and all the Russian Royal Family and Young Sam for the price of a pint, had not only returned to Hugeley like a bad penny but was moreover employed as a refuse disposal operator on the dust-cart. There was a shortage of labour and Moggy had so exhausted national assistance that in the end even he had felt yearnings for work and the Works

Department had overcome its reluctance.

Moggy was gingery red with lots of gold freckles. In his early thirties, he looked like the boyish hero of an American war-film but a hero gone wrong. He did not look you in the eyes and when he did he overplayed the look of candid innocence so that you became suspicious. He had so forgotten honesty that he could not act it correctly. Having the glamour of prison, he was popular among the other men on the dust-cart, and with his gift of the gab and freckled handsomeness he was popular with the housewives into whose yards he came, with the tread of a fox while they watched with keen eyes to make sure he took only the bin.

'He's just a bit light-handed,' they would say with easy tolerance (as one might remark on a child's passion for lemon-meringue).

But not so Young Sam.

Joe Hoyle, Young Sam's agent telephoned in the morning and called to receive his orders and to leave a large leg of lamb. He was instructed to obtain a bin for Underwood and to inform the Council that if rates were to be paid then the refuse must be collected.

'If you're near Underwood, you might see if the sty's in good shape,' Young Sam delicately suggested, 'and that t'watter's coming pure through the tap. Being a widow-woman, she'll happen need some help. I think she's a mind to keep a pig and some hens.'

Joe, who was married, made no comment. Young Sam pointedly did not ask after Mrs. Hoyle's health in case he was told.

By one o'clock Young Sam had the hounds patrolling the house, with all doors locked, and he took his position in a chair close to the window. The guns were within reach. He had a full view of the bins of The Lees, one for ordinary rubbish and the other for bottles and metal-containers which the Council, if they had their heads screwed on, should sell for re-processing. Nobody could have excelled Young Sam's patriotic zeal and loving care during the war in saving pig-swill, silver paper and cans, tins and old iron. He had not broken the habit.

Just before two o'clock there came the sleepy chug-chug and

patter of the council dust-cart approaching along the old pack-road which ran past The Lees. The road was maintained by the council and had a good surface but there was one little bridge that could take a maximum pressure dangerously near that of the dust-cart. There had been a protracted battle between Young Sam and the council over this but as the chief rate-payer he had got his way. The dust-cart was sent empty to The Lees; near the bridge the men who rode on the back of the cart got down and the driver with tender care edged the cart over. Then the men at the back mounted and others got in the cab and with a fine panache the cart glided in triumph to the gate of The Lees.

Here they made a terrific din, opening the metal lids of the refuse containers and shouting instructions to the driver to 'Whoa!' and 'Or-right!' as he edged the cart back to leave room for cyclists and pedestrians and to avoid knocking down the stone ball from the stone-shaft of the gate.

There had been another stiff battle fought over the correct procedure at the gate, Young Sam confronting the council as medieval kings did the barons. Alleging that there was a risk of damaging the stone-balls he refused to let the dust-cart back down the setts to his bins; the men were capable of carrying the bins to the cart *outside* the gate, in his opinion. He insisted that after the bins had been duly emptied the gate should be closed (in case cows or sheep wandered in). He further demanded that the bins should be replaced in a quiet decent manner, not with a republican clang. As usual, he gained his points.

The men seemed to make more noise than necessary, as if it were a war-shout they dared not fully release, and came clattering cheerful and obstreperous down the setts. Unobserved, Young Sam watched the invasion and, in particular, Moggy. What a shifty devil! He had on corduroy trousers tied with string above the big boots, and a khaki army jacket. Even in the big boots and the full afternoon sun he moved with the prowl of a predatory animal—a ginger tom with designs on the fish in the scullery—as if, even when walking straight, he was slinking around an invisible corner. His eyes were everywhere, dancing blue eyes mobile as dust in a sunbeam, looking for loot.

In the middle of the great tithe-barn was a demure col-
lapsible let-down metal screen painted white. Behind it was a
completely modern garage holding the old Rolls Royce and
another old-fashioned motor car in perfect condition, its big
brass headlights beautifully polished. Moggy was unaware
that anything of value lay behind the innocent-looking screen.
Young Sam had had the modern garage installed in the middle
of the medieval tithe-barn in the early 1920s; the ends of the
tithe-barn were still in the condition of stables and held old
carts and traps and old leather and brass horse-gear (all
steadily rising in value as the age of the horse receded). The
cars had likewise matured towards inclusion in an Automobile
Museum or a Veteran Car rally.

The presence of Moggy to within the precincts of The Lees
was a considerable affront to Young Sam who had not forgiven
the slander of the oxo-cubes and liked to have a large joint
under a meat cloth visible in the kitchen to confound Moggy's
inquisitive face. Young Sam was convinced that Moggy was
testing his defenses and, once finding a weakness, would break
in and cheerfully commit murder. A villain like Moggy would
not balk at leaving a time-bomb to blast his way into The Lees,
and anyone could see how his eyes lit up with possibilities
whenever they met a drain-pipe.

Young Sam watched every move. The more insouciant
Moggy was, the more suspicious became Young Sam. Each
bin was lifted by one man and another helped to support and
steady it. Moggy, lending moral support, had edged to a corner
of the great tithe-barn. Young Sam controlled himself from
sending a bullet through the window. Gazing at a passing
cloud, Moggy abstractedly dropped his rolled-up cap near the
corner, and moved away, one thumb in his belt.

The bins were brought back and set down with mock-
solemnity, one big chap daintily blowing on the lid as if to
remove a speck of dirt and pretending to rub it with his
sleeve. Then the men moved out of The Lees, Moggy dreamily
humming as he stepped with his gaze at the sky, and the iron
gate was closed.

As the dust-cart droned away, Young Sam was out of the
side-door and across to the great tithe-barn to see what it was

that Moggy had considered worthy of his talent—an open window maybe. The cap was indisputably there, and round the corner was the object that Moggy presumably prized enough to wish to steal: a white stone-mortar that Young Sam had found useful as a water-bowl for the hounds.

'He's after my mortar,' thought Young Sam bursting with rage and indignation at Moggy's dishonest impudence. 'He'll get more than he reckoned for if he comes back. There's nothing sacred to these heathen scoundrels.' He retired to the house, and waited.

Fifteen minutes passed by, and then the long freckled face, cold and calculating, of Moggy appeared again at the gate. He waited but, all being still at The Lees, he got over the gate and came quietly down the setts. He did a little pantomime of pretending first to look for and then locate his cap. He made for the corner where the cap was and bent down to retrieve it.

At this point Young Sam opened the side-door and the hounds exploded out, in a snarling streak arrowing to their human target. Moggy gave a high-pitched scream which resounded from Corbett Knoll, and there was a rending of cloth as the second and the third dog tore the corduroys in strips from him.

'Tha dirty thief!' roared Young Sam red in the face and rather dazed by the sudden view of Moggy's pale-white backside mangled with blood like something put through a mincer, with rags of corduroy flying. His face agonized and screaming like a kettle, Moggy fought up the setts and kicking and sobbing managed to scramble over the gate.

Young Sam found himself trembling and seismographic planes of darkness moved before his eyes. With his hand before him he got back into the house and sank in a chair, struggling for breath.

The back of his head ached but as he returned to calm he could hear the excitement of the dogs outside in the grounds, voices and the sharp clatter of stones. The voices rose in menace.

'It's not the dogs. It's that owld bugger.'

'Come out murderer.'

Stones sharply struck the outside of The Lees; a window

exploded into flying glass.

Moving slowly and stiffly, for there was a pain in his chest and his limbs seemed tightly tied by unseen cords, Young Sam groped his way to the study and asked the Hugeley operator for the police.

Downing the whisky, Sergeant Bilberry became even more red-faced than usual. He sweated comfortably, seated on the leather sofa in the study. Constable Boon who had accompanied him was somewhere in the grounds at the back of The Lees, having a look at the telescope and taking the opportunity of snooping through the windows.

'Moggy's a boy all right,' the Sergeant was saying in his pleasant non-commissioned officer's voice with which he charmed local criminals to make confessions and soft-soaped the local bigwigs and the inspectorate twelve miles away. 'A proper twister,' he said with some admiration. 'But he hasn't the brains for a big job. By himself he'll not get further than a bit of blackmail. He'll make the most of this, though. It's a good thing you made that call to me—it sort of covers you. He was foaming about charging you for attempted murder. Now, now, Mr. Ryder. Nobody can charge you for opening your own door and the dogs getting out. You weren't to know there was a trespasser. If his fingerprints are on the bowl as I reckon, then if it came to a court-case he'd not stand much chance. Still, it's nasty. But from what the doctor said it seems he'll have nobbut a scar on his bum. 'Course he'll play it up. I reckon you'd best have a word with your solicitor, just to be prepared.'

'What about?' said Young Sam sourly.

'Well, trespass is a funny thing in law. Moggy'll claim he came back just for his cap. There's his breeches—he'll want the cost of those corduroys in gold.'

'His breeches!' Young Sam exclaimed. 'Wasn't he planning at The Pale Apprentice to have me murdered?'

'Just burglary,' said the Sergeant. 'Aye, I will.'

'I suppose he'd like me to send him the keys to come up here and walk in and rob and murder me. Well, I'm old-fashioned: I believe what's mine is mine, and I'll let no thief come and take nothing of mine. I want to charge him with meditated theft of my mortar.'

The Sergeant scratched his chin. 'Now Mr. Ryder. It 'us be a difficult thing to prove, like. I've no doubt that's what he were up to. Moggy would snitch the wax from a corpse's ears. But with his claiming attempted murder and the cost of his breeches, there's ramifications, like. I reckon myself that it would make things a lot easier if he began to think of putting in a claim for industrial injury, occupational hazard, so to speak. There's no sense in rushing at this headlong, like. With the law it's go-easy, I always say.'

'All I want is my rights as a citizen. Protection of my life and my property.'

'Well, no harm's come to it as yet,' said the Sergeant bluntly. 'It's Moggy as is in hospital with his beauty blemished. You see old Hoggart, and, mark my words, he'll tell you what I told you. These trespass cases are tricky things. It's best for the present to stick to the plain fact that you came out of your door and before you knew someone was bitten. Let's keep it straight and simple.'

'I don't know · that anything's straight and simple any more,' sighed Young Sam. 'Principles don't seem to matter. We've got to be robbed of our mortars and not prosecute those who smash our windows. All this softness to the evil-doer— aye, I'll have a small one to settle myself—it fair takes away peace of mind.'

'Peace of mind . . .' sighed the Sergeant. 'Two more years, then my pension. The boy will be out of agricultural college by then.'

They started as a boney face appeared at the window. It was Constable Boon who having looked in vain through all the back windows in the hope of seeing the nude paintings and statues with which The Lees was reputed to be stocked was now trying the front ones.

'Ask him to come in for a drop,' said Young Sam hospitably.

'He's on duty and driving,' said Sergeant Bilberry, rising. 'Well, well, I'll be seeing Moggy and I'll let him know that if he steps out of line I'll get him for the mortar. It's all best kept unofficial. But in the meantime don't go using a gun. If there's any trouble, give us a ring. And I reckon if you fixed a warning on t'gate "Beware of Dogs" it'd put a good look on things.'

'I never thowt to live to see t'day when I sat in my own home afeared of thieving scum,' Young Sam grumbled.

Sergeant Bilberry gave Young Sam a glance which the old man, wincing, interpreted as meaning, 'You should have married and had sons.' So he should, but life and choice had not been as simple as the Sergeant liked to think.

'There's no call to be feared,' said the Sergeant kindly as he prepared to depart. 'It's just that with roughnecks it's best to leave protection to us.'

If he had felt fitter, Young Sam would have disputed the Sergeant's statement, but it had been an exhausting day and though the whisky had put some life into him he felt drained of energy. His arms seemed to be prickling. The sight of Moggy's mangled flesh had made him feel ill and when the window came in it was as if something had broken in his head. A good night's sleep, though should restore him.

With leaden feet he went down to the cellar to let the dogs out.

He would telephone Joe in the morning to come and repair the broken window.

His sleep was fitful, troubled with dreams of fire and policemen, the skies blood-red and the woods on fire.

which decorated the hard silk of the mane, and he seemed to hear the sound of brush and comb grooming.

Sometimes, coming out of a doze with his mother's voice vibrant and actual in his head, it was hard to tell what was dream and what reality. He could no longer tell in the ghostly house, and if he woke up with the night come and no lights on it was with the wonder of one newly dead.

On Sunday, though feeling a bit better, Young Sam did not attend the Harvest Thanksgiving Services at Rossall Church. He had earlier decided to boycott services which he considered as verging on blasphemy in the circumstances, and so his indisposition caused no inconvenience. As it had rained all summer and the hay had been spoilt, there was nothing to thank God for in Young Sam's opinion. What God chose to do was part of His mystery and no one complained, but to render thanks for stuff hardly fit for silage was mockery and would give the Almighty the impression that the churchgoers of Rossall Parish did not know their right hand from their left.

The present Vicar who had started adjourning after choir-practice with the choir to The Bottle and Blind Bagpipes, to the detriment of custom there, was not, in Young Sam's eyes, gifted with gumption. Vicars seldom are, but this one with his encouraging the parishioners to set up hand-looms and taking the choir pub-crawling was soggier than most. Moreover, he had appeared on television and was a Liberal.

In the afternoon, with a fuzz of beard and whisker over his face and wearing an old hat of his father's to save him from getting a cold in the head (so that he bore a close resemblance to Tommy Feather, the last of the real hand-loom weavers), Young Sam toddled out to the telescope. There was a roll of clouds to the West which promised to ruin the Harvest Thanksgiving if it hastened. He had expected a good rattle of hail, but thunder would do.

The paths of the woods were full of trippers.

'Litter, litter, litter,' said Young Sam to the sky.

Nature-lovers—the pale spectacled ladies looking for squirrels. Lovers—looking for nooks. 'Serves 'em right if an adder gets 'em,' thought Young Sam as the telescope located two pairs of shoes amid the bracken. Young men in short

shorts and mountaineering boots, hatchets in hand. 'To chop
my trees?' he wondered indignantly. Family groups—father
stalking morosely ahead, mother with one pram piled with all
the gear, grandmother at the back with two howling children
and the dog.

Starting fires, frightening the sheep and fish and all of them
going to be drenched before the day was out for not one of
them had an umbrella.

'Coming out into the country without a gamp,' thought
Young Sam. 'They think standing under a tree is the same as a
shop-door, till they're struck by lightning.'

But another cause of offence diverted his attention.

Traffic was discouraged in the woods, except that going to
the farms and residents on the way. The track was very
rough. There were signs at the entrance to the woods saying
the entrance was forbidden to vehicles except those to residents,
but country-lovers in cars were seldom discouraged so tractors
and breakdown cranes were frequently summoned to retrieve
motorists in difficulties. A spot where the Spring bluebells
bloomed bluest testified to where a Ford Popular like a meteor
had plunged over a crag and scorched a crater.

Passing the trippers in the rough road, a man on a bright
scooter could be seen buzzing along, and he was not going to
any farm for he turned on to the frailer track that led nowhere
except to Underwood. His head rose up and down and the
scooter like a shuttle went in and out as the trees hid him, but
all the time he was steadily advancing upon Underwood.

The cheek of the rogue!

There is something impudent and provocative about a
scooter as if it is derisively putting its tongue out at great
solemn cars and the Household Cavalry.

Young Sam glowered.

The scooter's rider was a big husky fellow with scorching
red hair, tight leather trousers and a highly coloured wind-
cheater with a bright neckerchief tucked inside. There was an
air about him—suddenly Young Sam recognized it.

'He's a-cooartin',' thought Young Sam, taking double
offence at all this colour and flaming sexuality rampant on a
scooter in *his* woods on a *Sunday*. A scooter does not suggest

honourable intentions, and it is a vehicle ill-suited to the gravity of the Sabbath day.

'Such carryings-on,' thought Young Sam feeling critical of the Almighty for not having put a stop to the young man's progress with a good downpour and growl of thunder. Instead he rode right up to Underwood, stopped at the door where Mrs. Fox tripped out, lips gorgeous with paint and her ears flashing like a chandelier, and opened the door of the barn for the scooter to be wheeled inside. Then the two of them, arm in arm, waltzed into the cottage and closed the front-door as the sky blushed black and rain roared down. The suddenness of the storm startled Young Sam who stumbled with his right eye taking the impact of the telescope's hard rim so that for a moment he saw stars and kaleidoscopic designs. A cold rush of air drove sideways into the open wooden-canopied way connecting the telescope-platform with the house, so that Young Sam shivered despite his long combs.

Truly the wind blows hardest on the just while those who are no better than they should be, stay snug in warm cottages.

Blinking his raw eye he made his way to the house with its dim bleakness and sad old furniture. Mrs. Fox might be a heathen but that was no excuse to behave like one. English widows were no longer so loyal as of old when they hid their hair with caps and sitting upright were never seen to smile again.

He decided to fill a hot-water bottle and go to bed. The gutters were gurgling and the windows running with rain; shrubs and trees dripped miserably.

A fallen world, thought Young Sam; unless the man were her brother. But even unbaptized widows are not given to putting on crystal ear-rings to greet a brother, unless perhaps it is one returning from abroad. But that fellow had never arrived from overseas, not on that scooter. He did not have the look of a man who was capable of having sisters.

A tumbler of whisky with a drop of hot water would help to keep the cold out of his bones. He frowned as he observed how little whisky was left in the bottle. In future he mustn't be so free in offering it to his visitors, not at the price it was nowadays.

Of course with her being just registered, she would not be

likely to worry about sinning as she was a lost 'un from the start. It was really up to the Vicar but he was more likely to talk her into going in for a hand-loom.

Young Sam sighed comprehensively over the price of whisky and the difficulties of transforming Mrs. Fox at the font from pagan Peggy to Christian Margaret. She must be baptized and made human!

CHAPTER FOUR

From Underwood on the last day of September, Young Sam's stumpy figure could be seen coming along the leaf-strewn path. His sharp glance seemed to be noting which leaves had been misbehaving, or calculating how much the fallen boughs might fetch as firewood. The badgers stayed quieter in their earths and the squirrels did not descend the trees.

'Someone might crack their skulls,' Young Sam muttered, lifting a banana-skin from the path with the ferule of his umbrella.

He had shaved so that his face glowed smooth pink and he looked like a cross baby. He was in clogs and a solid pair of moleskin trousers. His shirt was of collarless flannel from the undisposed stock of the mill that had closed down in 1914, and over this he had several old pullovers and a moleskin waistcoat to hold his pocket watch. On top he had the grubby old mackintosh as he believed in dressing for the weather, and resembled a bulky sphere as he moved like a Noh actor in his clogs. He stopped.

But the sound was not from a bird, a trapped rabbit or collapsed cow. It was man-made and came on the winds from the open door of Underwood.

'Why hello, Mr. Ryder,' cried Mrs. Fox coming out with her head swathed in a gold lamé turban and a shovel in her hand. 'You are looking well! I did appreciate your sending the bin. How you think of everything—my word.'

'Where's that noise coming from?' demanded Young Sam abruptly. 'It's like a fair-ground here. . . .'

'My favourite,' cried Mrs. Fox, chanting a little of the music, which was 'Hullo Dolly'. 'Aren't I a lucky girl? I was lucky enough to get a battery radio—I really did think I would have to do without music. Ssh!' She lifted an arm like a traffic policeman and hushed Young Sam's opening mouth. 'Oh isn't it heavenly? Liberace!'

'If I only had the gift,' said Mrs. Fox with loud wistfulness after Young Sam, startled, had stood in cenotaph silence till the piece ended. 'I would love to play an instrument. But we can't all. . . . Oh!' She sniffed vigorously and with a cry darted back indoors. 'My scones! Do come in, Mr. Ryder. Pardon my manners. Sit down if you can find a place.'

Young Sam hesitated at the door of the cottage, cleaning his clogs on the sack outside but reluctant to go trampling in clogs on the cottage's red-tiled floor. He was pleased to see how well she had brought up the colour and produced a gleam. He stepped out of the clogs and entered in his stockinged feet. Mrs. Fox was bent before the oven and with a dishcloth retrieved the scones that were done.

'The worst of this oven,' she said straightening up with a heat-flushed face, 'is that you can't control the heat.'

She had the oven-door handle gleaming with Brasso and had blackleaded the door itself so that the patterned surface of oak-leaves, acorns and mice shone sleekly.

'It's a pretty looking door. There's few of them to be seen nowadays,' said Young Sam.

'Oh the door's well enough. But the oven's a proper antique.'

'Aye, so it is. I've been offered fair sums from these collectors,' said Young Sam seriously. 'Mind you, it's only seventeenth century—it's lasted well. They didn't make things flimsy then. I reckon the original is under this—you couldn't call it an oven. The meat would hang on a spit and the fire was low down. You could have sat inside the chimney then.'

'No thanks,' said Mrs. Fox pouring boiling water on to the tea and setting out two plates. 'I prefer to sit outside the fireplace. The bottom of the oven has a crack in it; I've covered it with a sheet of iron. I'll butter your scones for you—I don't know how they managed in the seventeenth century but, even with bricks in, this grate just eats up the coal.'

'They used only wood.'

'They must have spent all the time sawing it then.'

'So they did—so they did. And got so warm chopping the wood they didn't need no fire,' laughed Young Sam. 'Mm— there's few things so pleasant as a hot scone flooded and sopped with melted butter. It's as light as a snow-flake. Hm, there's magic in such pastry.'

'There is,' said Mrs. Fox with the firelight flashing in her golden eyes. 'It's my mother's recipe. But the oven can't be regulated. I suppose they hadn't invented flues and ventilators for ovens then.'

'They'd use a bake-stone afore this was put in. You don't get scones like this from an electric oven. And there's always this to remember—you don't get electricity for nowt.'

'I have to pay for the coal, you know.'

'Then use wood.'

'But it's the work of sawing—and one has to buy a wood-saw.'

'A good wind sometimes brings the boughs down in just the right size—that batch is done now—Can I see the crack?'

The heat of the oven blew out as the door was open.

'The iron plate is red hot. The crack's underneath,' said Mrs. Fox looking for the long tongs to lift up the metal.

'Tut, tut,' Young Sam said observing the crack through which smoke streamed as soon as the glowing iron was lifted. 'The oven's fair busted. But 'appen,' he said hopefully, 'it could be mended for a small sum. There's always hope.'

'Do have another cup,' said Mrs. Fox lifting up the tea-pot which was of red clay with black incised Chinese characters.

'You make a good cup,' Young Sam commented, his eyes taking in the room.

'I was planning to whiten the kitchen ceiling,' Mrs. Fox said noticing his glance towards the open kitchen door. 'The ceilings do get black with the lamps.'

'Who looks at a ceiling?' said Young Sam. 'A black ceiling doesn't get dirty but a white 'un does. I'd lime the walls if I were you. It kills any creepy-crawlies and keeps t'place cool in summer. You don't want any fancifications,' he said looking distrustfully at a few framed reproductions on the walls.

'They're van Goghs,' said Mrs. Fox.

'Ah. Well, you can't beat a case of stuffed birds and a case-clock, I always say. How's the lavatory?'

'The . . . Oh, the earth-closet? It seems all right.'

'I hope the can hasn't corroded. There isn't the same

workmanship nowadays. You want a good iron kettle here.
These aluminium things are nowt. When you've had 'em a
week, the bottom's gone. They can't stand up. They colour the
knobs different, but I'm not taken in. This Swedish hardware
now—I'd rather use my fingers. No, you don't want fancifications in this nick of the woods,' he said glaring again at the
van Gogh's. 'All right in France, I dare say. Let them have red
knobs on their kettles and Swedish hardware. But give me an
iron kettle and my cutlery from Sheffield. A fork which looks
like one, with honest prongs!'

'I don't see what forks have to do with my paintings,'
protested his tenant.

'It's all of a piece,' said Young Sam. There's some folk as
should hang,' he fiercely recollected Moggy. 'Keep an eye on
your bin-lid, especially at weekends as some of these trippers
'ull walk off with anything. We had one fellow taken up at
Pilney for taking t'bin-lids from six farms. He was one of these
London beet-necks, lived in a cellar and hung the walls with
bin-lids. And a bin without a lid. . . .'

'Is like a man without a woman,' Mrs. Fox finished quietly.

'Eh?' Young Sam blinked.

'It's a popular song. "A man without a woman",' intoned
Mrs. Fox demurely, her golden eyes laughing coquettishly, 'is
like a ship without a sail.'

'You could say the same about a woman,' Young Sam
answered undisconcerted. 'But it's a lot of modern tripe, in my
opinion. There's some as paddles along best on their own. Miss
Winterbottom was my Sunday School teacher—a very good
woman. She was comfortably off—in the North Eastern
Railway and the Suez Canal. Always knitting and tatting and
sending away parcels to the Gold Coast, and out every morning
with soup and baccy for the distressed. She loved committees
and auctions and rummage sales. Died at ninety-eight with
every tooth in her head. She was very fond of Annie S. Swan
but of course not on Sundays. There was never a happier soul
on earth and if she had made the mistake of marrying I doubt
her light would have shone so far. And there were no red-haired
men calling at her house on scooters! There wouldn't be so
much sex in Britain today if it weren't for the radio and

television and these American and French films and popular songs. Yeh, yeh, yeh! If people worked harder they wouldn't have the time and strength for all this football and sex.'

'I'm sure,' Mrs. Fox declared with a flash of white teeth, 'that I am free to receive a visitor whether he comes on a scooter or not. And if you are implying Mr. Wildman is a footballer, he most certainly is not.'

'Mr. Wildman! Is that his name? I asked my agent who the fellow could be calling on Mrs. Fox, but Joe couldn't make out either. We thought he must be from Pilney, maybe.'

'I don't see that it is any concern of yours, Mr. Ryder,' said Mrs. Fox coldly, 'but Mr. Wildman happens to be a gentleman from Australia. He knew the late Mr. Fox, and he has a small farm on the Midgeley hillside.'

'From Australia, eh?' said Young Sam, in no way abashed. 'I thowt he had long legs.'

'He has very kindly offered to charge my battery for me,' said Mrs. Fox with dignity.

'Well, if I were a young widow woman,' said Young Sam, 'I would be very very careful afore I let any young man from Australia come charging any battery of mine. Mind you, it's uncommon kind of him to come all this way to be obliging, but I'd keep him out on the doorstep.'

'In the teeming rain?'

'In a snow-storm,' said Young Sam firmly. 'You're a woman, and he's not only a man but from Australia where the sun is hot.'

'You know, Mr. Ryder,' said Mrs. Fox with a charming little laugh as she swished over the hearth-rug with a slinky Dietrich rump, 'I do think you are just a teeny bit jealous of Mr. Wildman.'

'Nonsense!' said the old man with a sudden loss of his usual bluff conviction. As Mrs. Fox had moved he had become aware of the close animal femininity. He struggled to forget what he had felt. Such tight dresses shouldn't be allowed. 'Nonsense! I've one foot in the grave. January shouldn't go wedding with May. If this Mr. Wildman hasn't got a wife in Australia (as is highly improbable), no one would be more pleased to see you arm in arm together going to be lawful spouses—if it takes place in a Christian building and you've been sprinkled and given a Christian soul in baptism.'

'Mr. Ryder, he has come only to charge my batteries and here you have me at the altar.'

'One thing leads to another in this world,' said Young Sam with morose experience.

'I can tell you now,' Mrs. Fox enunciated, 'that I'm not so willing to be tied as you are to imagine me in church. There's a lot to be said for being a freelance.'

Young Sam looked thunder-struck. 'I never thought to hear those words from a woman,' he said faintly. 'Do you imply you want to be a common courtesan?'

'After you have digested my scones,' Mrs. Fox flashed, 'that is a nice thing to say to me. But a widow learns to endure the cruel insults of a cruel unfeeling world. You men have such terribly filthy minds, but you religious ones are the worst. No one would have called me a courtesan in Manchester. They don't know the meaning of such language!'

'Now, now lass,' said Young Sam, breathing heavily. 'It wur yourself as talked about being a freelance. I've not meant to reproach you with anything above being a heathen, and I'm being straight about that. If t'Vicar won't come out with it, I will. There'll be time to worry about your eternal damnation when you've got owt to damn. You needn't be among the babies,' he coaxed. 'I'll have a word with t'Vicar and we'll arrange a dark night just for yourself . . .'

Mrs. Fox laughed.

'You won't be laughing when we go up in glory and you have no hope of grace at the final account.'

'Oh Mr. Ryder, I'm thirty-eight and I've seen cruelties galore. You will have lived through more than I, and do you really think there will be a final accounting and redress of the miseries and injustices of our existence? Those who were roasted alive or hacked and hunted to death, their agony is not one whit the less for your pious hopes and gloss.'

'I like to hope there is something,' said Young Sam glancing at the night gathering outside and back to the fire.

'Weakness and fear lie behind your beliefs, and help to hide you from yourself. You are frightened to look behind your mask.'

'And do *you* know yourself?' he demanded fiercely.

'I know better what I am than you what *you* are. But we are getting very serious,' she laughed. 'It would be too soon and sudden for us to start removing our masks just now.'

'I think you've shown me a bit of your true self.'

She merely smiled.

'Well,' said Young Sam taking out his watch, 'It's coming on dark uncommon early and I've no torch. So I'll be making tracks. I've enjoyed our conversation. You're a headstrong lass and it'll do you no good, having them notions. I can't make you out, and that's a fact. But you make good scones. They were a fair treat.'

'Take some with you.' She was already looking for a paper bag.

'It's kind of you—I won't say no.'

When Young Sam was at last in his clogs and mac, umbrella in hand and scones in pocket, he peered at the garden: 'Ah— so you've put in some taters!'

'No, they're flowers—biennials.'

'Something to eat would be more sensible. Nothing like a fresh-grown vegetable!' he trumpeted.

Mrs. Fox sighed softly in the dusk.

Young Sam crossed Crush Water by the old stone bridge. The water chuckled over the shallow bed below. He glanced back up the valley to where the cottage stood nestled on the hillside among trees. There was the light, a little dancing dot at this distance. As he watched it swelled and grew brighter—a small globe that seemed to squint off and dance higher up in the air, then shrinking, skip back.

'She's not trimmed t'wick,' Young Sam muttered wondering. Then he seemed to see two lights—then quite a group of small flashing globes and night-lights like marsh will-of-the-wisps. He rubbed his eyes with a knuckle and when he looked again there was just the only little steady light of the cottage.

He was seeing things, he told himself, from straining his eyes by looking a long time in one place.

He began the long haul up the hill path to The Lees.

CHAPTER FIVE

With meticulous lack of speed Young Sam drove his polished old Rolls Royce down the hanging main street of Rossall. The main street was of a construction earlier than the Domesday Book and at its bottom made a turn so abrupt and severe that even the canniest horse was not safe. However, Young Sam made the turn successfully and braked before the three long black and gilt embellished windows of Josiah Ramps and Sons.

Formerly, from its strategic location, a smithy had stood here and the Ramps had been blacksmiths for many generations. But in the eighteenth century the Jo Ramp of the day had been converted from hard drinking, profane speaking and lewd living by the Reverend William Grimshaw and business had boomed. The present three generations of the Ramp family, who all served in the shop, were as noted for the soundness of their church principles as for their merchandise. They supplied machinery, hardware, cutlery, fireplaces and baths to the local farms, and their goods were designed 'to last'. Their buckets were stout and galvanized; they did not descend to plastic. The firm was not without its literary connections, for early in the century W. B. Yeats had purchased a pocket-knife from old Mr. Ramps who with unfailing honesty had to inform research-students from the United States that even if the knife had been the one used to cut a bough for wandering Aengus he regrettably had no recollection of the poet's voice or appearance as 'we get a lot of Irish in here, mostly in the summer.'

Young Sam made his purchases at Ramps' because their stuff was durable and their cement solid. Today he intended to purchase a new fireplace and oven for Underwood. Hitherto not given to lavish modernizing of his property, he had been moved by the gift of scones and the sight of the old cracked iron oven to surprise Mrs. Fox with a brand new tiled fireplace and the best coal oven that money could buy. He particularly wanted a tiled fireplace to spare Mrs. Fox the labour of black-leading an extensive surface.

Today only the young fellow was available in the shop. This was Josiah the grandson, in his early forties and regarded with some suspicion by Young Sam not only on account of his youth but because he had had a 'fancy' education at Oxford. He had studied ancient Greek at great expense but failed to enter the Foreign Office. Young Sam resented the air of 'knowingness' on every topic the young fellow had picked up while pursuing his ancient Greek.

As if to commemorate the lavish spending of money, Young Sam was in a clean shirt and a well-pressed suit of the best Yorkshire cloth—but he had not shaven. The Ramps did not rate the wasting of a blade.

Young Josh was very tall and thin, with a consular nose registering a fine scorn for the barbarian world. He was wearing a dark blue overall like an imperial toga and holding a ball of putty as if it were the Orb of England. He took in Young Sam's entrance without a smile and silently adjusted an advertising board for Wilkinson Sword razor blades. The sarcasm was not lost on Young Sam who bluntly enquired, 'Is nobbut thee 'ere?' and on hearing it was so, said resignedly, ' 'Appen tha'll do then. Tha can sell a fireplace, I hope.'

'Please step into the showroom,' said Young Josiah in his precise posh voice.

The showroom lay behind the third shop window and con-sisted of the third shop opened into a room behind. Models of fireplaces were everywhere and some had been cemented and fixed as working models. Young Sam opened oven-doors and peered critically inside. Josiah stood tall and silent with sardonic nose.

'Well, I fancy this 'un,' said Young Sam surveying a hand-some tiled affair with a large oven on its right side.

'The disadvantage of this model,' said Josiah, 'is that under excessive heat the tiles drop off.'

'Drop off? Isn't it made properly then?'

'The model gives every satisfaction. It is by a leading maker. I was merely venturing a personal observation from experience. A model in which the tiles are supported by a wooden or a metal frame is, in my experience, ultimately more satisfying if the oven is in constant use. In this model the tiles are unsupported and under great heat are likely to drop off.'

'If any tiles drop off this 'un I'll be having summat to say to the manufacturers. The oven's a good size for a goose.'

'For a goose?' enquired Josiah with distaste.

'Or a turkey, or a good batch of loaves. These here other ones will hold no more nor a rice pudding. I'll take this one.'

'So be it,' said Josiah with resignation so intense it became imprecation.

'And I suppose you'll arrange for it to be installed. But I want a discount for the trade-in of t'old model. It's right good metal.'

'What make is it? There's no demand for the old-fashioned type of range nowadays.'

'It's not rightly a range. You could sell it to one of these Harrogate dealers for a mint of money—to put in one of those ultra-modern old-world cottages they build. Willy Bryan got a mint for those owld beams of his cottage when it was demolished. There's a big demand I hear in Washington and New York for old things, and you won't see an oven like that every day. Mind you, it's got a crack in it, but that won't matter if it's in a museum. The Americans could fix it up a bit if they wanted to be cooking their hot dogs in it. You can't rightly expect it for nowt.'

'Well, Mr. Ryder, without seeing it I can't say and I would have to ask my father.'

'Aye, well, do. And there's a bit of a hurry to this. I want new fireplace in afore the weather becomes real smeaking.'

'We could start the day after tomorrow.'

'Do you mean you'll be coming yourself?'

'Well, I'll have to have a look to estimate how quickly the men should be through.'

'Oh aye. Well, give me a call on the telephone and we can go down together.' Young Sam hesitated. 'And the workmen— are they—reliable and married, oldish men, you know? Safe to leave alone?'

'Percy and Herbert? Percy's about fifty and Herbert's forty. They're both married and I suppose reliable. We've never had any complaints. I'm sure they are absolutely honest.'

'And, of course, I'll be keeping an eye on things,' said Young Sam as if speaking aloud to himself.

Autumn drove through the valley, whooping the leaves into great whirlpools like ostrichs' nests, scraping and violining till naked blue sky showed where green curtains had been before, and the rocky understructure of the land with caves and cliff-faces could be detected beyond the bare thrashing boughs. Pelted with flying leaves, Young Sam daily trudged along the cornflake-crackling path to Underwood. He wore a big tweed cap pulled down over his ears, a muffler, a woollen overcoat with the moleskin waistcoat over his jumper, and the inevitable clogs. He had always been adjured in youth to 'wrap up well' and the winter's Siberian nip could be felt already in these October blasts. They razored his cheeks to a boiled ham pinkness and his nose harmonized jollily with the last rowan-berries.

It was after an early mid-day dinner that Young Sam set forth for Underwood and so caught the best of the day on his walk there. Arriving around one o'clock enabled him, moreover, to see what progress Percy and Herbert had made in the morning. They had spent two days dismantling the old fireplace and smashed it to smithereens in the process. As a result Young Josiah had estimated two pounds for the pieces as scrap metal, but Young Sam refused to include the oven-door at this price. The brass-handle alone was worth more than that and the door itself was a fine example of seventeenth century domestic art which any folk-museum should rejoice to possess.

The original medieval hearth had been laid bare behind and under the later iron grate and oven, and Mrs. Fox who had complained of the chilliness had made temporary use of this medieval hearth for her cooking and warmth on the second night. Young Sam had stayed a bit later that evening and had two potatoes baked à la medieval hearth while he had explained how you could sit in the chimney-place and be snug. He had had to keep his overcoat on as he sat on a stool and looked up the chimney at the stars in the sky's black marble for the draught of the open space was quite freezing and Mrs. Fox in a chunky woollen sweater remained unconvinced about comfort of the medieval ages. She wanted the new modern grate in as speedily as possible, and Young Sam did not wish the work dragging on till Saturday afternoon when Percy and Herbert would extort overtime.

Arriving at the cottage, Young Sam found a big puddle of cement outside, sacks and newspapers laid on the red tiles within and the new fireplace in position but not completely fixed and cemented. There was a gap of about twenty centimetres all around where the new fireplace did not reach the stone surround of the original space. Percy and Herbert were now wedging this space with stones and bricks which they would cement over. At their feet was a pile of golden and crimson leaves that had fluttered down the chimney while they were working; some were pasted to their big boots.

Young Sam scrutinized the work, to see if any tiles had been marred or cracked, but the fireplace had been brought carefully muffled in soft cloths and straw and there was no damage for even Young Sam to detect.

In the barn, Mrs. Fox in a golden turban carelessly fixed with an imitation ruby the size of a duck's egg, so that she looked like a fortune-telling sister of Carmen Miranda, was boiling an egg on the old boiler which in the old days had been used for heating the pigs' mash. Wisps of her gold-red hair had slipped wantonly from under the turban. She had on a tight red-rust sweater and (where Young Sam's eyes moved, troubled, from the ruby then back again) tights of drab olive green.

She looked a proper heathen.

'You want good thick bloomers on you this weather,' said Young Sam in a crabbed voice from the doorway. 'You can get your death of cold parading around in Yorkshire like that. We're not the South of France here, you know.'

'It has not escaped my notice, entirely,' said Mrs. Fox tartly. 'They were a bit more gallant in Manchester, come to that.'

'Fine words butter no parsnips,' said Young Sam obscurely, withdrawing to the company of Herbert and Percy who showed their resentment of his inspectorate by the set of their backs.

Percy wore a big-buckled belt and Herbert braces. Both had

on thick flannel collarless shirts. They were stocky men with broad moon faces of those parts of the West Riding where the Danes had settled. Though their countenances were expressionless, their brief non-committal answers and their resentful silence were eloquent of their dislike of Young Sam. Later in 'The Pale Apprentice' they would joke coarsely, pints in hand, about that 'owld bugger'.

Young Sam was in fact trying to make himself as pleasant as possible by trying to yarn, during the men's break about the two World Wars and the old game-keeper who had lived at Underwood. But Percy and Herbert, though almost tempted with camaraderie by the topics of war and local pride, would have none of it. He was not one of them. He did not have his cards stamped and if he were ill he would not be in the ward of Pilney General Infirmary but in some posh nursing home.

As if to symbolize the divide between them, Mrs. Fox served the working men mugs of tea and sandwiches on one tray and brought Young Sam a cup of tea and his sandwich on another.

The fireplace was finally cemented in place and the clean unsooted fireback had its neat surround of still wet fireclay. Herbert and Percy waited outside in a corner of the field, for the small lorry to come and fetch them. It was part of their work agreement with Ramps that they would be carried back to Rossall each night by motorized transport.

After the men had gone Young Sam lingered. The evening sky was blackening, lowering with a few golden streaks. He felt lonely now that the work had come to a full-stop and he no longer had an excuse to come across to Underwood. He surveyed the cold new fireplace and felt the chill of the cottage.

Herbert had given solemn adjurations not to light a fire over the weekend—the cement must dry out thoroughly.

Lingering awkwardly (for he could not very well stay on for another meal) Young Sam was inspired to say, 'Well, I'll look in on Monday just to make sure the cement's dried satisfactorily. . . . I hope you won't be starved of cold this weekend . . .' he commiserated.

'Oh I'll manage,' said Mrs. Fox with her enigmatic smile. 'I've some fur. And I'm ever so grateful to you for giving me the nice surprise of such a beautiful modern fireplace, Mr. Ryder.'

'If the chimney only draws,' hoped Young Sam gruffly, and on that note departed.

As he dived into the darkness of the woodland path, he could hear the saucy cheerful strains of a foreign—possibly a French —song blown to the night and stars from Mrs. Fox's battery radio.

She could have been born in France, he mused. That would explain the lack of religion and turban and slacks. There had always been lots of foreigners in Manchester. And the French. . . .

As usual he paused on the old stone pack-horse bridge. He saw lights dancing in the wood, but these were headlights dancing in a forward direction. He could hear the pip-pop of a scooter.

It must be that Wildman fellow on his way to Underwood to charge her batteries.

The trees were lit up and all was plunged again into darkness.

Every night after dark a scooter flooding the trees with light had passed towards Underwood. Young Sam had not heard the scooter departing. No battery radio needed batteries charged every day, unless she were very wasteful. Serve the pair of them right if they caught their death of cold in the unheated cottage. . . . Such goings-on were all very well no doubt in Manchester and Paris, but Rossall Parish had its reputation to maintain.

CHAPTER SIX

At six month intervals, Young Sam sitting alone would experience a great clarity of mind in which the universe and its inhabitants would appear to him under a new light. Whenever he was afforded such momentous illuminations, he would either summon a member of his firm of solicitors, Warmer and Warmer, or go down to Hugeley in person and CHANGE HIS WILL.

Ever since the death of his mother he had been perfecting the disposal of his estate. Some items, such as the bequests to his old housekeeper and to Joe Hoyle, had remained constant, but all else fluctuated. At present the bulk of his estate was to be shared by the dogs' home at Pilney and the Lord's Day Observance Society—he having been overwhelmingly convinced six months ago of the merits and needs of dog-welfare and stricter Sabbath observance. He had left the parish church enough money to buy a new lightning conductor.

But now the universe suddenly assumed a new aspect. What were the well-lined bellies of dogs compared with a human soul? If they had too much money, might not the crusaders for a truly godly Sunday lose their present fervour?

One could endow a society for the baptism of hitherto unbaptized adults in England and Wales. There must be scores of such creatures lurking in the parishes, and thousands if one counted also the Chinese, Pakistanis and gipsies whom the winds of chance had blown to these islands.

It was not enough for vicars passively to receive infants brought for a sprinkling; it was necessary in the modern world to go out and drag in those adults who had somehow escaped the net. The Christian Name Society—that was what his society would be called. No more Peggies. No more Betties. The aim would be a fully baptized Britain.

'And I hereby leave, devise and bequeath the sum of two

thousand pounds to Mrs. Margaret Fox, commonly known as Mrs. Peggy Fox, widow, and the life-tenancy free of rent of the cottage known as Underwood to the said Mrs. Margaret Fox, known as Mrs. Peggy Fox, widow, should the said Margaret Fox, known as Mrs. Peggy Fox, widow, present herself at Rossall Parish Church and submit to the rite of Christian baptism, and should the said Mrs. Margaret Fox, known as Mrs. Peggy Fox, widow, fail to present herself for baptism at Rossall Parish Church within two years of my death, then the above bequests of two thousand pounds and rent-free life-tenancy of the cottage known as Underwood shall be considered null and void.'

That's the stuff, thought Young Sam. Dreamily he fell to musing whether he was not perhaps over-generous in providing the church with a new lightning-conductor. Perhaps money for the overhaul of the old one would be wiser? Or might it not be more 'saving' in the long run to increase the annual insurance-coverage on the church edifice?

He took a sheet of foolscap and in his old-fashioned clerkly hand wrote the draft of a new will which he would get Warmer and Warmer later to make proof against invalidation. However drear and damp the weather, the evenings always raced for Young Sam whenever he had the delightful task of reformulating his last will and testament.

He struggled, sick, out of a dream. They had come to a hotel, his mother and he, and had entered for lunch. It was a grand hotel, like the old railway hotels in London, and his mother had passed into the dining room, but in the lounge he had felt his chest whelm with blood and the red stuff had spilled out of his mouth. The manager, hotel servants and a woman hotel-receptionist with a familiar face had swooped down on him, not to succour him but to put him out of the hotel before he disgraced their hotel with blood and the taint of mortal sickness. How politely firm they were in propelling and carrying him to a taxi, leaving him faintly to murmur 'Hospital!' while his mother, knowing nothing of his plight, waited within. All the blood in him was oozing out—this was death. And his mother, so old and helpless, would never know what had befallen him. As he fell to the floor of the taxi he strove to breathe out a command, and in a sickness of horror awoke.

But it wasn't true—only a dream, and yet the same pain was in his chest and the same nauseated fear. He was slimed with sweat. He pushed away the coverlet.

There was a wild almost full moon glaring through the glass. He breathed heavily, taking in the relief of its having been merely a dream, till he began to feel cold.

A vixen howled—the shrill sound seeming so close that he judged there must be a frost on the hills. Downstairs the dogs jumped and growled. There was thin ice on the window-pane.

Why had he been dreaming of that hotel, he wondered, and why had the feeling of the dream been so evil? He did not remember ever having gone to such a hotel, but sometimes he had taken his mother for an outing by car and perhaps they had stopped for lunch at such a hotel.

The vixen cried again—a lonely exulting ululation.

His mother had been dying then. Now it is I who am dying. The dream is of my death. And that taxi was my hearse. . . .

The moon was sinking when he again opened his eyes after an unrefreshing sleep. He was not restored at all; the pain was still a dull ache in his chest and his mind seemed in a thousand fragments. But he knew sleep would be impossible.

His feet as he put them out of bed to find the carpet-slippers looked blue, and he could not now tell if this was the effect of the moonlight or the condition of his veins. His arms when he rolled back the sleeves of his nightshirt were stained with small dark red spots. He was tired too in an absent way as a clock might feel if all its works were out. As he shuffled, panting a little, to the window, he felt just a shell.

'Well, well' he muttered, calming himself as he thought how his father must have felt the same, and all old men. We all go through it; we all come to it, baby-cap and school-cap and young men's hats and on to the head-covering of the corpse; the round.

A piece of the river gleamed like a sickle-blade in the darkness of the river. Silvery clouds rushed in tumult over the black breasts of the hills. He could make out no light in the darkness where Underwood should be.

In the morning he would have the new will made neat and his duty would be done. Though there was no need for a will, or much of one at least, if. . . . Only once had he intended marriage, and his mother had intervened. True, Annie was a nobody. But she would have bred; he would have kept her family off. Some sons would have followed their own course, despite 'honour thy father and thy mother'. His mother had wanted him to marry and had brought girls of the right families to The Lees, but it was only Annie he had ever wanted. But never enough to anguish his mother. Wives, after all, abounded; there were agencies to supply them. But a mother was unique.

Horses and dogs did not supply the place of a son, or a daughter even. 'I have no child' slowly echoed in his thought.

Even now it was not too late. Had Mrs. Fox been baptized. . . . A woman of her age was capable of bearing.

Abruptly the moon flared like a candle over the knoll and went out.

At the sight of his employer's exhausted white face and puffed eyelids on the Monday morning, Joe Hoyle for once insisted on advising Young Sam, and Young Sam thinking that one more visitor would make little upset, grumblingly agreed to see a doctor. Though you paid them money only to tell you what you knew already.

Dr. Johnson, who arrived after Warmer had left with the new will, declared that Young Sam had a tired heart and would need a week or two's complete rest. Young Sam looked sour enough at this for he knew damn well his heart was tired. The doctor's intention was for Young Sam to avoid all activity —he must stay in bed.

Joe volunteered the services of Mrs. Hoyle. 'She'd be only too pleased. . . .'

'I've no doubt she would. It 'ud be a week's rest for you, Joe. No, keep her out of here. She clacks so.'

There was a scarcity of suitable women if Mrs. Hoyle's services were spurned.

'Mrs. Fox is a tidy sort of body,' Young Sam began, looking a bit redder in the face.

'People would talk,' said Joe solemnly. (His wife certainly

would if a strange woman were given the free run of The Lees in preference to herself.) 'And she's not a qualified nurse.'

'She's a champion cook, Joe,' said Young Sam.

'But you need a professional nurse if you're to stay here. Dr. Johnson suggested a nursing home or a proper nurse coming in. I could look after the place myself if it was just a matter of extra help being needed. You've got to have your pulse felt and the thingumibob in your mouth, you know.'

'Well, you'd best look in every day, Joe, to see that the dogs are fed and watch what the nurse is up to. Living in other people's houses I suppose they'll turn their noses up at pigs' trotters and expect caviar at every meal. Try and get a plain sensible Yorkshirewoman, Joe—with a taste for homely food and a good punch for that Moggy if he starts any of his tricks when he comes for the dust-bins. He'll be looking for a chance to make off with summat once he hears I've a tired heart.'

'I'll keep an eye out for him, don't worry.'

'I don't hold with this staying in bed at all. It makes one worse. But I don't feel too good and that's the truth. . . . Porridge and kippers would be a good idea for the nurse, with potatoes. Nourishing too.'

'I'll order some.'

'You can't beat a good kipper. Better than all that caviar muck,' came dreamily from the invalid.

CHAPTER SEVEN

Nurse Crook recommended by Dr. Johnson, came from Harrogate and worked at The Lees for three weeks. A gentle philosophical-looking red-faced woman, she showed no symtoms of distress at anything Young Sam said, but in the kitchen and her bedroom kept her transistor invariably set to a pirate station and showed a great partiality for potted meat which she took on Ryvita with a bottle of Guinness. She unbent so far as to inform Young Sam that she had always been a Christian and an orphan, and Joe Hoyle learnt that her name was Ethel and she had a pen-friend, also a nurse, in New York. She confided that in her judgment The Lees was 'a bit of a museum' and mysteriously added that 'there's a lot of it in Yorkshire.' She was fond of *The Mikado* and Bing Crosby, but did not think the Beatles 'true music'.

She also struck up a friendship with a big black tomcat that mysteriously appeared in the field and was coaxed into the kitchen. In Harrogate, she explained, she could not keep a cat because of her budgerigars.

Young Sam, strictly confined aloft, was aware neither of the cat nor the immense leap in his next electricity bill. The Lees blazed on its hillside every night so from the prodigal expense of light local opinion knew Young Sam must be dying.

The Vicar of Rossall called three times. As the pair knew each other so well, and disagreed totally upon all earthly things, the Vicar confined himself to the reading aloud of the Bible from the point where Young Sam had stopped and to passages from the Prayer Book. The invalid initiated more general conversation by obtaining facts and figures about the insurance coverage on the church in the case of fire or its being struck by lightning. The Vicar found it difficult to remember the precise details of the more minute knots and he was rather peeved at his rich parishioner's evident dissatisfaction with the present insurance-coverage.

'If God out of his inscrutable wisdom does smite us,' said the Vicar loftily, 'we are not aiming to make a *profit* out of it.'

Young Sam declared he had never seen the sense of hand-looms and a dead loss on everything, either. Bored with being in bed, Young Sam could not wait till he was dead before the question of the lightning-conductor was settled and he brightened up as he computed to the final three pence the saving in having the present conductor overhauled rather than a new one installed.

'Mr. Ryder,' said the Vicar with restraint. He was a middle-aged man, straight-backed, with an aureole of silver hair and a pleasant T.V. manner. 'We are unfortunately not a poor church. We are, in my opinion, over-endowed as Rossall seems to have produced more millionaires or near-millionaires per square yard than in any other parish, and the church has benefited handsomely. All our needs are met, and there, in my experience as a pastor, is a great stumbling-block. The social work of a parish suffers grievously if there is no call for and demand upon unselfish service. There is a blight upon that parish which has no need of a jumble-sale or a bingo-evening, and feels no pressure to raise funds by the joyful occasion of a whist-drive. Allow me,' he said, raising his hand, 'Such is the situation in Rossall Parish. We are suffocated with funds. There is no cold spur of necessity and want in our fat flanks. And you are proposing to deprive us even of a natural disaster; you will not allow an act of God by affliction to rouse us from our stupor of too generous and closely tied endowments. Sacrifice—that should be the slogan of us all in Rossall Parish—sacrifice, my dear Mr. Ryder.'

'Excuse me, Mr. Ryder,' said Nurse Crook appearing after a knock and a cough, 'but you have another visitor. Aren't we popular today? A lady who has called with some lovely chrysanths—Mrs. Fox.'

'I'm just on my way,' said the Vicar. 'Mrs. Horsfall is in need of comfort—her leg gets no better and there's been no news of her grandson.'

'Pot-holing should be outlawed,' pronounced Young Sam, rallying from the snub to his wealth.

He found it strange and somewhat disturbing to have Mrs.
Fox scented and pearled in his bedroom, a place where he had
little dreamt she would ever appear. Nurse Crook fussed in the
background with a couple of vases, not knowing whether the
blue or the black would be better, but Mrs. Fox thought the
blue would go well with the golden chrysanthemums.

'I'm all for vivid contrast,' she declared forcefully.

'They remind me of coffins,' said Young Sam fretfully,
'though lilies are worse.'

'To me,' intoned Mrs. Fox, 'chrysanthemums are flowers of
passion and pomp. They are regal and put me in mind of old
Japan.'

'I like the old tea-roses,' said Young Sam weakly.

Mrs. Fox was hatless but had a sort of net of spangled
artificial pearls over her flaming red hair. She had drop
ear-rings and a necklace also of pearls. Her dress was of dull
brown velvet but her appearance, as Young Sam took it all in,
was far from dull. He would not have called her exactly a
scarlet woman, as she could not be held responsible for her hair
but she seemed rather lacking in subdued widowhood. Her
legs were englamoured in nylon stockings that harmonized
with the brown velvet, pearls and red hair, and gleamed in the
firelight. Young Sam's eyes did not move from them. He voiced
his disapproval of the elegant high-heeled flim-flams which did
service as her shoes.

'A pair of clogs 'ud be more saving,' he said. 'Them things
will wear out on the stone in half a week.'

'What seems a luxury to you men,' said Mrs. Fox with a
light throaty laughter, 'is a necessity of life to us poor women.
Clogs, shawls, red flannel and W.R.A.C. bloomers must wait,
Mr. Ryder, till I go on the old age pension. And if you must
know a woman's little secrets, I came here in flat heels and
changed into these before I came upstairs.'

'I've never met anyone like you,' said Young Sam with
conviction. 'Except once in the pantomime at Bradford when
the leading girl wore the same as that thing you've got in your
hair. In real life I mean—nay, I don't know if you're real.
You're a bit of a glamour-puss and no mistake.'

'Well, I'd rather be a glamour-puss than a Maggie Block.'

'If only you were baptized. . . . You've got the Vicar frightened of you. He went out like a weasel as soon as you showed.
He's a funny devil, the Vicar, and no mistake.' Young Sam fell
to brooding how the Vicar had more or less intimated that he
did not want more endowments for the church and seemed to
think church socials would be stimulated by having the church
burnt down.

'I am afraid,' said Mrs. Fox softly, misinterpreting his
preoccupation, 'that it was very thoughtless of me to come
intruding on you when you are so weak. But I was anxious and
wanted to show some esteem for your kindness with the
fireplace.'

'Has the cement dried?' Young Sam vigorously asked.

'Perfectly.'

'Lot of rubbish Young Ramp talked about the tiles dropping
out! As for me I never felt better. They're keeping me up here
as long as possible to swell the bill. But she's a good nurse, I'll
say that for her. Christian to the core. If she hadn't been
baptized she would have sunk. Born an orphan but look at her
now—a nurse with her own flat and . . .'

'Well, I haven't done so badly,' Mrs. Fox protested.

'But you don't know what's around the corner.'

'Who does?'

'Oh you mightn't feel it now but you'll feel it then. . . . Like
a dog that hasn't been vaccinated,' said Young Sam vividly.

'Oh pooh. I don't believe it makes a scrap of difference.'

'The rabies of sin—that's what it is.'

'I do wish you'd let the subject drop.'

'It's your immortal soul you're neglecting to take precautions
for.'

'I haven't got one,' said Mrs. Fox.

'Now, now come,' said Young Sam peering with his red-
rimmed eyes over the cold chiselled fold of the white sheet,
'you're not an animal.'

'Perhaps I am,' spoke Mrs. Fox pettishly. Stricken with
remorse and embarrassment, Young Sam saw tears brim from
the corners of her golden eyes and trickle, mingling with the
face-powder, down the sides of her nose.

'Forgive me, my dear, 'said Young Sam. 'It's the way we

speak here, and I'm not used to young women. I can't change now. You know I'm going to die soon, don't you? So make allowances for an old fellow. I've been marred, you know, by having too much. The last of the line. Yes, I'm the runt. They were long-livers, the old Ryders, but I'll not see even seventy. The race *is* to the swift. There's truth in us before we die. Human life's a messy affair. Two wars, and a third coming up. The whole creation groans—so if we cannot reach out and find a mercy beyond, what is there for us but agony?'

Mrs. Fox had turned to the fire while she dabbed her eyes and repaired the powder. 'And don't you think it's worse,' she said in a low tone, 'for the creation which wants to be human but isn't? You have everything but are not happy. I wish I had been brought up in a house like this.'

Young Sam gave a sigh and said, 'The grass is always greener on the other side of the fence. I was an only child. I used to think what a wonderful lot they were down at Underwood. I could leave you the house here, you know,' he said in his short sharp way, 'but it 'ud be no different from Underwood. Just more to worry about and keep clean.' He was on the point of saying more—the words 'You know, you ought to have children, lass' forming in his head and about to come from his lips—when seeing Mrs. Fox's face, repaired after its shower, he was reminded that he was addressing the softer sex and requested more softly instead, 'Will you pull the bell? Ay, that big porcelain knob. The nurse can bring us a pot of tea. She's got nowt else to do.'

'I've brought you some fairy-cakes and scones made in the new oven,' was Mrs. Fox's only comment as she pulled the bell which creaked rustily as it came out and twanged back.

'Ah,' came from Young Sam in pleasure as his visitor unknotted a bandeau and from it produced a box containing dainty little cakes, iced and un-iced, and rough triangular scones.

Nurse Crook brought in the tea on a silver tray. Mrs. Fox had moved a side-table nearer to the bed. Young Sam had declined to have the electric light switched on but suggested that the fire be stirred up. In the flicker of exaggerated shadow and light, with the silver distortedly mirroring them and the blank white winter dusk in the window, Young Sam and his visitor drank tea and ate the cakes and scones brought as a present. The firelight shook red and gold from the figure of Mrs. Fox.

'Is that a ruby ring you're wearing?' asked Young Sam from the darker farness of the bed.

'I've no ring on today,' she answered.

'Eh, haven't you. . . . What was that flashing?'

'Sparks up the chimney, I expect.'

'They're magical little cakes, these,' he munched.

'I'm so glad you enjoy them.'

Mrs. Fox's tone of voice had, as so often, changed to the prim and demure, with a hint of light mockery perhaps. One could not be sure, but her great golden eyes seemed to be smiling, in that peculiar way of hers. Was it craftiness or sadness, or what? This inscrutable semi-smiling expression as her eyes flashed fascinated Young Sam as he gazed at her haloed in the firelight. With all the velvety fire-colours of her hair and attire she seemed to merge into the flames, and with gleaming engoldened in nylon legs her vanishing up the chimney did not seem too improbable. Young Sam gazed drowsily.

The fire had sunk to a little red glow and no Mrs. Fox was there. Annoyed, Young Sam assumed that he must have dozed off in his visitor's presence. There was a strange little jigging sound to be heard inside the house in the early winter's night.

Far-off in The Lees Nurse Crook's transistor was tuned in to Radio Caroline.

In the dark valley under Corbett Knoll a vixen howled.

The next morning Young Sam had the senior partner of Warmer and Warmer's brought to The Lees and in a new will he left the bulk of his fortune to Mrs. Fox, provided that she undergo baptism in the parish church of Rossall and, in place of 'Peggy' assume the Christian name of Margaret.

CHAPTER EIGHT

Nurse Crook was seen no more at The Lees; Doctor Johnson no longer came. All had gone back to normal, with Joe Hoyle his henchman coming at his master's bidding and the dustmen making their collection every Monday.

But there was a difference as in these late days of November mist hid the valley below The Lees. In the thin wintery sunshine of some of the afternoons Young Sam, in a thick navy-blue woollen jumper and serge trousers, with his clogs on, would saunter, helped by a stick, from the house up the setts to the big iron gate. His complexion was a rich red. He liked to exchange greetings with the few tenants passing along the lonely road and they were all impressed by the unusual affability. This softened manner and his slowness of movement led to the general verdict: 'The old man hasn't got long left.'

As soon as the sun began to drop into the moors and the first night-cold invaded the air, Young Sam crept back into the house. For two weeks he moved no further than to the gate and just lingered in the little late sunshine, as the cicada trapped in the ventilation-shaft of a house can be heard singing when all the others have gone. The moors and knolls of the Pennines lay bald and bleak. Soon the first snow would speckle the black wastes of Walshaw and Oxenhope. Wintery emptiness was everywhere, and the stout old stone houses, so few in number on the hill-tops, were stark silhouettes in the sky's void.

Making only gentle exertions daily, Young Sam felt deep content. The sudden new testamentary disposal of his estate gave him a sense of catharsis. He felt that in the best way possible he had ensured the continuity of The Lees. It had been a ticklish will to make law-proof, for he had wished to ensure that no future husband of Mrs. Fox should get his hands on any Ryder money or property, and in the event of Mrs. Fox refusing to become Margaret the estate and monies would go to the parish church. But the lady, who had with such naive sincerity voiced a wish to have been born in a big house, was scarcely likely to refuse The Lees and a liberal income.

'And I shall be snugly under my slab,' thought Young Sam almost gaily. A lonely childless old man past sixty can be allowed some indulgence in the pleasure he derives from a spacious final disposal of his possessions. Now that his will was finally settled, he felt free. The emptiness of sky was his home; he was released from the bondage of possession, and gratefully taking the sunshine on his face in his daily stroll to the gate, the last of the family was in his new-found poverty not so unlike those first Cistercians who had had their grange here where the tithe-barn and The Lees now stood. The awareness that death could not be so far off, for he read daily in the mirror the cardiac over-health of his face, brought also a blissful assurance of reunion: he would join his dead in fellowship, the last guest of his group, for whom they had been waiting.

The peace of the early winter landscape reflected the land of his soul. The vital sun was daily shrinking, and the pale heron quested over the silent fields into the mist.

On awakening from sleep, though, with the voices of the long-dead fresh in his ears, he could remember the last most recent events of the strange dreams that came nightly. He knew —with intuitive conviction—that these dreams were messages from the realm of neither time nor space. In the calm of early morning, as a dead leaf grinded and whispered on the stone of the outer wall, he tried in vain to recall the soundless music of the stately dance to which figures in great red masks had solemnly moved. Had it been a dance or a ritual? The mask had been vermilion, large and distorted, and the robes of dark gold. He could recall the white-socked feet falling as softly as snow. The figures in the baggy unlife-like robes and great masks had been tall and solemn as gods. Who these great masked figures were that had danced through his dream he did not know; were they like idols or high priests of Baal, he wondered, or, if the masks were removed, would he recognize them?

Joe Hoyle brought the meat for the dogs as usual. At night they had the run of the house and on rising Young Sam would

let them out into the grounds. Later they were tempted back to
their kennels in the cellar. Taking them their evening food,
Young Sam became aware of a strange listlessness in his dogs.
They were much quieter, so that at first he had the sensation of
becoming deaf. Then he wondered if by some peculiar sympathy of sense they knew that all was not well with their
master. They were eating normally. Perhaps, after all, they
merely felt the semi-hibernating influence of winter and were
less lively than usual.

Young Sam had been looking forward to a second visit from
Mrs. Fox, but the second week of December was drawing on
and she still had not appeared again at The Lees. This was a
disappointment for Young Sam who could not help feeling that
his heir, even an unknowing one, owed him especial con-
sideration. Moreover the rent for Underwood was due.

Crush Valley had been obscured for weeks by sluggish mists
so that even with the telescope what was going on below under
the lagging mists remained impenetrable. Young Sam was left
as frustrated and baffled as an astronomer wanting to know
what is actually happening beneath the Venusian clouds. Had
Mrs. Fox caught a chill? Had she fallen from the steps while
whitening a ceiling and lay now unconscious and helpless on
the back-kitchen's stone-floor? Or had some pimpled adolescent
or an older desperado like Moggy Greenwood bashed her on
the head in order to obtain her post-office savings book?

It was very strange and worrying.

She ought to have called.

The rent was due.

Of course, Joe Hoyle could have been despatched down to
Underwood if it were only a matter of money. Young Sam was
a bit offended, and a bit worried too when the district was full
of desperate characters like Moggy who were always more than
usually avid for money near Christmas-time, but more than
anything he wanted to gladden his eyes with the glow of her
presence and to savour his own personality in the clash with
hers.

Suddenly at three o'clock one afternoon in the middle of
December he put on a cap and overcoat, his muffler and gloves,

and stepped into his clogs. After some deliberation he fetched a stock. It was a long haul back. . . .

The dogs were in the cellar, strangely quiet. He decided he ought to let them out and descended the stairs, but when he opened the door they did not hurl out. They were listlessly lying about. They recognized him and began to rise. He determined to summon the vet as soon as he got back; they had not even finished all their meat. Had they a vitamin or mineral deficiency? There was no smell of gas or any external reason for this unusual lethargy.

He left the door open for them and troubled at their puzzling lack of spirits went up the stairs. But before going out he telephoned the Hoyles' cottage and asked Joe to come to The Lees and arrange for Mr. Rogers to inspect the dogs as soon as possible. He himself expected to be back about five.

Concern for the dogs had, by association, intensified his concern for Mrs. Fox. She could well have fallen a victim to sickness, and if Wildman and the post had not called. . . .

He turned into the clough, the ravine which descended precipitously into Crush Valley. The path wound its way down to the old stone bridge over Crush Water. The valley was thick with mist, and once in the clough he had to pick his way carefully. He was glad he had brought the stick as this gave him added safety. The mist was so thick that at times he could not see two steps in front of him and the stick told him whether there was solid ground or empty air with rough crags and the side-stream below. Ahead, unseen, he heard the loud rushing of Crush Water, like the shrill crying of millions of spirits. The main stream which rose far-off in the moors was greatly swollen in winter. As he came closer to the old bridge, he saw the bare wire-like twigs of the bilberry bushes shaking from the agitation of turbulent waters below. Foam piled thick behind giant boulders. It was as if quiet Crush Water had become an angry brown animal frothing with rage.

On the other side of the bridge, Young Sam turned through the woods in the direction of Underwood. Tyre-tracks had been made in the soft ground and water and dank leaves had filled the ruts. Below, the river roared and shrieked so that the ground seemed to shake. Mist twisted slowly through the bare trees and flocked against the hillside. From rocks capped with poverty grass moisture dripped on to clumps of sphagnum moss. Everywhere silly weak voices seemed babbling, mocking —non-human voices. Young Sam stopped and mopped the sweat on his brow with his gloves. He had the feeling he was in one of his sinister dreams. The egg-faces of fungi on a log of fallen wood appeared malevolent. He felt as hot as if it were a muggy day in July. The standing still cooled him, and breathing heavily, he moved forward again.

The roof of Underwood came into sight. At once he noticed that there was no smoke from the chimney. He had a terrified intuition that all was wrong, and his heart burst.

The cottage had no appearance at all of human warmth; no atmosphere came from it of life or human sound or footfall. A great stain of green moss on an outer wall spoke of damp and spreading nature. The chinks on the low roof were swollen with saturated yellow and green moss. As he slowly advanced to the gate, he saw that the windows were blind with mist. About him was the silence of the mist, the remote thunder of Crush Water and the weak bedlam of voices of rivulets and drops. His breath was louder than all.

The little white gate sagged as if no one had passed through it for years; the wood had rotted and came apart as he made it yield. The wetness and mist gave the cottage a look of utter neglect.

He knocked, but no one came. From the quality of the silence within, an emptiness reverberating to infinity, he knew that no one would come or could ever come. He knocked again but he might as well have rapped on the door of a grave.

He felt himself turning dizzy with possibilities. He steadied himself on the latch, and the door whined open.

He saw at once that the tiles were glazed dully with moist film, and the rotten closed-up air of the inside offended his nostrils. All was dulled and damp.

In his clogs he had moved forward a few steps, and he saw the new fireplace which he had had installed. Two tiles near the top of the front had come loose and lay smashed on the hearth. The black of the oven was filmed with moisture. His gaze travelled to the old wall-bed of which a panel was open.

He could see the dirty heap of the mattress which he had believed he had witnessed Mrs. Fox burning. There were no pictures on the walls; nothing indeed to show that the cottage had recently been under human occupation.

But in the nauseating atmosphere he knew it was not ghosts that had been present here, not normal ghosts who linger immaterially at scenes of old happiness or unhappiness. Nor had it been tramps or trippers who had slept and eaten within the damp walls. The stink within the cottage was real and overpowering and it was not human but animal. He had stood within many farmyards but never till now had he experienced such an intense odour of animal bodies pressing together—the odour of animal waste more revolting in the domestic surroundings. There was the stink of foxes everywhere. The dim cold rooms had been the abode of foxes.

As in a vision Young Sam saw again Mrs. Fox's face, this time grinning at him, and in horror of the inexplicable he broke away from his own thoughts and stumbled out of the cottage. He hastened back along the path by which he had come and as he drew near to the stone bridge the waters seemed to hurl shrill taunting maddening voices at him. He was very hot and wanted to get out of the steamy stifling mists as soon as possible. Every so often the overpowering stench of foxes seemed to be pouring again into his lungs, and he dug his stick furiously into the ground to climb up the rise of the clough more swiftly. He was panting and out of breath; his eyes were swimming and he felt as if a railway train were roaring through his head. He wanted to get back to The Lees at once and call Warmer and Warmer. His whole being was constricted with horror at the disgusting pervasive animality of the things that had been in the cottage. He had no awareness of how rapidly, with crab-like ungainliness, he was ascending the clough. Once on the main road, perspiring and dizzy he turned in the direction of his house.

As he swayed at the gate and managed to open it. Joe Hoyle came out of the side-door and up the setts. His face spoke disaster. 'The vet's been. It's a bad business,' he began. Young Sam stood panting, unable to frame words.

'He couldn't make it out but thinks it was a virus. He won't know till the autopsy.'

Young Sam just stared.

'They're all gone, Mr. Ryder,' said Joe gently. 'You're not looking too good. You shouldn't have gone walking uphill so soon.'

'Get me Warmer, quick Joe,' said Young Sam thickly—his voice seeming to himself as if it were coming along a tube. Joe supported him into the house and telephoned at once for the solicitors and Doctor Johnson.

Two cars were parked on the great driveway of stone setts.

At dusk all the lights of The Lees were on and in the bright windows of the study through the leafless trees figures could be seen moving to and fro.

Warmer drew up a new will leaving the bulk of the estate to the local church. The interest on the money, as Young Sam had proposed once before in an earlier will, was to be used exclusively and in perpetuity for a complete and extensive insurance-coverage for the church edifice and for the acquisition of a thoroughly up-to-date and scientific lightning-conductor and fire-prevention and alarm system. Few cathedrals in Europe were to be as well-insured as little Rossall Parish church.

Half-an-hour after he had penned his signature Young Sam expired, his eyes wide open as if in surprise.

When the bequest was announced, the Vicar did not conceal his vexation at this blow against the bridge-club and the social spirit of little humble sacrifices which a church deficit and tottering finances do so much to encourage.

He came out sharply in favour of the widow's mite, but this was without reference to Mrs. Peggy Fox who indeed was never met with in those parts again.

Nightingale Island

CHAPTER ONE

I take an interest in the after-careers of my pupils. The strapping hulks for whose English I was vigilant when at the age of twenty I began teaching in North Wales became either poachers or policemen. Nowadays in Japan I find that those who are extraordinarily hopeless and cannot pronounce 'Good morning!' in English will become teachers of English. This at least ensures their survival; a flicker of life will be maintained.

As for myself, I am haunted by the thought that if all my former pupils would contribute only ten pence a week to a fund I could be bought out of English teaching for ever. I read every Christmas of appeals for crippled children; there are advertisements for decayed gentlewomen and out-of-work television actors, but none of my old pupils has ever had the initiative to get going a rescue-fund for me. I am not eligible for a pension from either the Japanese or the British Ministry of Education, and the Ministry of Pensions warned me when I was eighteen that I need not expect a pension at seventy unless I was a more regular purchaser of stamps. One of my calmer dreams is of the ruler of England graciously bestowing an annual pension upon me, or the President of the United States (I know no national boundaries.) Such thoughts have become more frequent with me since I became thirty-five last year.

This might not seem a venerable age in Europe but in Japan it raises me to the status of a minor Confucius. Young ladies come to me for grave and suitable advice about their lovers' tiffs and whether they should accept mother's choice of a husband; tram-conductors call me 'Papa-san' and young men who will not stand even for a woman pregnant with twins, bow me to their seat when I am going only one stop. If I go to buy a hat, the shop-assistants foil my attempts to buy one with a perky feather by producing some dowdy affair from the shelves, as more decorous for my age.

All my dignity of age is increased if some passing pupils should address me as 'sensei' (twice-born) and cry rapturously 'Sir!' to prove their English lessons were not in vain.

I am often asked to give talks on such subjects as 'Should The Young Today Have More Moral Education'? or 'The World in My Time'.

Under the wisdom of thirty-five years and the burden of being pensionless (which is like being stateless), I was impressed by some paragraphs in The Japan *Times* about a Japanese teacher who was approached by a former pupil. Hiroshi, the ex-pupil, was running a bar and being in difficulties he proposed to his old master that they pool brains and go safe-breaking together.

Lucky teacher! None of my ex-pupils had ever come to me with such an interesting proposal. That teacher, too, was thirty-nine years old, which might well be considered advanced old age. I had a three years start on him when it came to shinning up drain-pipes or jumping from upper windows. I was still capable of giving the police a run for their money if I ever had a pupil of sufficient enterprise to prod me. Car-stealing was closed to me, however, as I could not drive, but basic elementary burglary, surely I was not too superannuated to add one more skill to my Anglo-Saxon, Middle English and Latin? Even if I proved a failure (like the example before me), I might use the three years hard labour in Yamaguchi Prison to write a best-seller. *Three Years Hard In a Japanese Prison*—it might be made into a film if I could train mice or the wild geese coming to perch outside my bars.

Of course the British Embassy would be annoyed, but as it was now they were not exactly pleased. They had sent me a Christmas card for my first Christmas in Japan when it was too late for me to rush out for one to send back. My failure to reciprocate must have caused offence for they never sent me another for all the subsequent Christmases. I was blackballed. Three years hard in Yamaguchi Prison would have seemed to them all you could expect of a fellow who did not send a Christmas card to the Embassy of his fellow-countrymen.

From my prison-cell I could correspond with a Japanese female pen-pal. . . . Her name could be 'Midori'. Audrey

Hepburn could play her and Peter O'Toole me. With the film-rights for *The Dividing Wall: Three Years Hard In a Japanese Prison* I could snap my fingers at the Ministry of Pensions and send the Embassy a Christmas card from Hollywood.

But I had no ex-pupil starring in the world of crime to inspire me, and the sad reality was that I was more likely to see the inside of a Japanese prison for the ill-paid stony work of teaching English to the inmates. Even the prisoners in Japan are eager to learn English or, rather, to boast that they have had English lessons. But could I not write my best-selling masterpiece without actually going to gaol? It could be in the third person. Anyone who has been teaching in schools for sixteen years surely knows what prison is like, save that the peace of a cell would be hard to imagine. Some of the parents I had known, especially the religious maniacs, could supply hints for the more depraved 'screws'. Once the end of term examinations were over, I would buy some note-books and commence *The Dividing Wall* if I had any strength left.

In the morning post there came a letter from Tomoshige Endo.

CHAPTER TWO

How well I remembered that thin smiling-eyed curly-headed youngster so smartly dressed when I first encountered him in a bar. I did not remember him from class because there were fifty of them, all dressed in identical black uniforms with brass buttons like shabby ships' stewards. However, when he had introduced himself as my pupil and told me his name, I instantly recognized him as the author of the best essay from any class of his year. The essaylet was entitled, 'My Ambition'.

An American educator at Sapporo had advised the young men of Meiji Japan to be ambitious. 'These are wonderful words,' wrote Tomoshige with charming frankness, 'and I am a very ambitious Japanese boy. I want to get married very quickly to an attractive Japanese girl. But I regret to say that our girls do not have such big busts. Japanese girls make very faithful wives and I too would try to be faithful but I do not think I can succeed as I know I can love more than once and a wife would be busy with the babies, of which I want six. But Japanese teachers of English do not have much money and as I also want a car and a big house with a different scroll hanging in the alcove every month I must struggle hard so that my children can be fed and well-educated. Therefore, I shall strive hard to find something which will bring me much money for family instead of living like the poor English teacher in "I Am A Cat". I also am ambitious to drink much whisky, to which I am inclined.'

The bar to which I had drifted that night, driven by the intolerable stress of holding an evening class for customs officers, to disgorge precious money on alcohol, was, of course, a cheap one with the pretty name, I remember, of 'The Three Lazy Samurai'. Tomoshige was not in student uniform but a well-cut suit with a lively silk tie. In excellent English he at once proposed going 'ladder-drinking', and when I explained

I had not so much money he said he had plenty as he had not only received remittances from his father and an uncle but he had also been paid that day by the rich parents of a dull child to whom he was teaching mathematics and in addition he had won six thousand yen at mahjong.

He plied me with drink till I was putty in his hands, and I remember the evening as a magic carpet tour whisking in and out of little bars full of black-eyed kimonoed girls, who were sometimes boys—floating down neon-lit little alleys, eating *o-sushi* at clean wooden counters and supping Chinese *soba* from thin bowls with red and gold key-patterns. I do not remember how the evening ended although I recollect the sensation—or is it a dream?—of chewing the leather of a Japanese taxi's seat and finding it mainly plastic, but when I woke up I found myself in a narrow crib-like bed with a wire-mesh about a foot above me. Tomoshige had brought me to his lodgings and was sleeping in the top bunk while I was in the lower. He provided me with his electric shaver and after a breakfast of hot-cake, which he made, he departed to his first class and I to mine. All day I had the taste of the taxi-seat and his hot-cake in my mouth.

He never asked a question in class. In fact I never remember any Japanese student asking a question except once in a lesson about British history when an anonymous voice demanded from the back of the class, 'What about old Ireland?' But in the bars he was the smartest student I ever had. We often went drinking together—in the cheap bars unless one of us had a windfall—and in the four years before he graduated I was grateful that there was one student in Japan whose conversation was not limited to the tea-ceremony. As the tea-ceremony is the most refined element of Japanese life, students think they impress one with their refinement by making the tea-ceremony the invariable topic of discussion. It is a theme of limited scope and not capable of variation, but refined. Tomoshige was principally impressed by the poverty of English teachers and secondly by the poverty of teachers in general. It was a topic which woke chords of melancholy statistics in me. He told me he would never teach in an urban high school as on the day of the leaving ceremony modern pupils were apt to turn up with knuckle-dusters to deal retribution to teachers whom they had particularly detested. 'The pupils in country schools haven't hitched on to this yet,' said Tomoshige wisely. 'A Country school is safer.'

He was married the day after graduation to Yuriko, one of the girl-students, who looked very attractive to me, though he was still full of laments about the smallness of Japanese females' breasts even on the eve of marriage, and I drank the wedding-*saké* in a flat saucer while the priest joined him in wedlock according to the Shinto ceremony. (Tomoshige being a staunch atheist but Yuriko determined to wear the wig, white cap and full kimono of a Japanese bride). Through the window of the train bearing him off to a honeymoon in Atami I thrust my parting present—a bottle of Old Parr while the railway loud-speakers played 'Auld Lang Syne'. There were quite a number of newly wed couples on that train as it was the last day to collect a tax rebate.

CHAPTER THREE

About a year later I received a Christmas card with a photograph of his first baby (a girl) and a letter in which he wrote that he and his wife were both teaching English at high schools and that after his first *Bonenkai*, the party to celebrate the semi-annual bonus, he had been so drunk that he had taken the wrong train home. He mentioned that most of his fellow-teachers were heavy drinkers but that as the youngest he was expected to drink the most.

Three years later came another Christmas card with a photograph of a family group (Tomishige wearing heavy spectacles and a waistcoat with a watch-chain) and inside the card he had scribbled that he was at a school in the Izu Peninsular. 'It's rather flea-bitten but the fishing is good,' was his comment.

After that I had heard nothing and for me he had merged into the forgotten past until the new Christmas card with its accompanying photograph of six stalwart children posed in front of a beautiful house reminded me that Tomoshige was still going strong. With the card and photograph was a longish letter on notepaper with a printed address:

MITSUBACHI,
UGUISU ISLAND.

I puzzled over this—was the house called 'The Honey-bee' or was Mitsubachi the name of a village. Uguisu Island meant 'Nightingale Island'—one of the remotest islands of Japan where a number of ex-Emperors had been exiled in the remote past. It was about as far from Kyoto as one could get and the ex-Emperor Gogo had died from excess of joy when a dumpling from his beloved Kyoto reached him on remote Nightingale Island. There are a number of Noh and Kabuki plays about Nightingale Island and the salient feature of life there, as imparted by the plays, is of remote bloodiness.

In the Noh play the old courtier Banjo has been so long on Nightingale Island that he has forgotten human speech (till towards the end emotion at the sight of his old master's sandal wafted by the sea-gods to the shore providentially restores it) while the chorus mournfully intones:

> When will I spread my fan
> To the breeze of Mount Hiei again?

In Kabuki plays the heroines, after poisoning many rich protectors in order to obtain money for the young and handsome but impecunious Himoroshi, are frequently transported in chains to Nightingale Island. This poor devil of an island is, in short, the Japanese Australia but worse as its horrors are never exactly defined. There are veiled allusions to such things as a lack of plum-blossom and possibly a lack of ink as letters from the Island are in drama, verse and romance written only in tears.

Tomoshige's letter, however, got over this shortage by being solidly typewritten and it started with the rapturous invocation:

'Most treasured Sensei, my old Mentor!'

The letter was written in a gust of enthusiasm as Tomoshige movingly recounted how fine and enobling had been my influence during the dark depression of his student days, but how at last he had come through storm and struggle to a ten-room house of his own on Nightingale Island where he was the headmaster of Uguisu College. 'But my happiness is not full until my old revered teacher comes to behold it. Please say you will come and stay for a long holiday with us. My wife has learnt to make scouse for your breakfast and you can stay in bed all the time except for excursions to the crater and to the grave of the ex-Emperor Gogo.'

With the years I had grown wary of accepting invitations anywhere in Japan as I had the inveterate habit of getting lost. Once I had been de-frozen in the mountains at a Zen nunnery and there was scarcely a little village-station in Chugoku where I had not rested my head on the platform through misreading a Chinese character in the time-table and arriving on a cattle-truck at three in the morning. I could not trust myself to get to Nightingale Island, wherever it was, and besides could I afford to go away for Christmas? But also, could I afford not to go away for Christmas and the New Year for if I stayed everyone would expect presents and cards?

Ah! Why not turn on the gas, climb into bed and have done with the weary battle against poverty that leads only to unsuperannuated pensionless old age?

I rose to the hammering of the postman on the door. There was another letter, a registered one, from Tomoshige. A collection of tickets piled out as I unfolded the letter. He wrote that he appreciated how difficult I found the Japanese way of obtaining tickets and so he had bought them for me, and he was including a map. I was to travel on the central railway line and then change, taking a branch-line Eastwards to Yumi City. To obviate my getting lost during the change of trains, he included a set of Chinese characters which would be on the branch train and at the barriers as well as a map of the station. There would be a further change at Yumi City but I need not worry as he would be there to meet me. He proposed our staying overnight in Yumi City before travelling the rest of the way to Nightingale Island. I was positively not to worry as there would be scouse for breakfast every morning and Yuriko had also managed to obtain two of the tins of haggises which had been circulating in Japan ever since the British Exhibition in Tokyo in 1965.

With my train-fares paid right up to Yumi City, I felt excited as if I were already travelling. I would need to take at least eight presents, but it would be cheaper than remaining. But what was all this about scouse for breakfast, and at Christmas too? I had never relished cold rice and seaweed for breakfast, but I was undemanding and a good cup of tea sufficed. Tomoshige must have discovered that scouse was the main dish of my native Liverpool and intended to pay me a delicate compliment, but scouse for breakfast! I hoped tinned haggis improved with age as the British Exhibition had occurred some years back. Still, it was no use worrying about food or one would go nowhere in Japan and the jellyfish of Nightingale Island were no doubt delicious. I would face them when they came.

Then I remembered my dog. Could I bribe one of the neighbours to take charge of him? But all the neighbours had big frothing hounds and alas! all my neighbours knew my Kumi. Though outsized by every dog in Japan, he had the true samurai spirit and sprang at the throat of every other male dog and ravished the bitches. Of course I could leave him to roam the streets till I returned, but the dog-gangsters might net him and sell him for vivisection. No! Even Kumi must be spared that and would have to travel with me—There was no help for it even if I had to buy a ticket for him, if there *were* tickets for dogs in Japan and if I was able to master the procedure of obtaining one.

Then what would I wear? In Southern Japan one seldom really needs an overcoat and this is just as well when a flimsy little sportie coat costs thirty pounds, but Nightingale Island was more northerly. I would have to wear my English overcoat which was sixteen years old and, being in the old English fashion, flowed about me and lent me a look of Ahasuerus. I examined it carefully but though the threads were thin they were nowhere broken and the moths had disdained to bite it. I would wear my best pair of plastic shoes till I got to Yumi City and then I could change back to sandals.

I would pack just a few shirts and pairs of socks and a supply of notebooks to contain: 'The Wall that Divides: My Five Years in A Japanese Prison'. On Nightingale Island I could get down to some serious work on the masterpiece for Metro-Goldwyn Mayer and Tomoshige could be jogged into providing some information on prison-diet. Perhaps in his capacity as headmaster he could arrange for me to make an educational trip around some local gaol. Were prisoners allowed a transistor radio in their cells? Tomoshige must research for me.

On second thoughts I packed a tin bowl and some sea-weed biscuits for Kumi. If he was semi-starved on the journey he might be more tractable.

It was then that I noticed that Tomoshige had considerately purchased a ticket for me on a train departing at five a.m. It is a time-hallowed custom for Japanese to start on journeys and day-excursions at incredible hours in the middle of the night or pre-morning, according to which way you look at it. Very well then. I would stay up all night to catch the train, and I would sleep during the journey.

Before I even got to the station I became aware that Kumi was going to be a considerable incumbrance. He is a cross between a spitz and a dachshund, with the colour of one and the elongated body of the other. Trying to hold him still is like grasping an eel. When any attempt is made to put him on your knee, he grows excited in the belief that he is about to be tickled. The damage was done, I believe, in the first few weeks of his childhood before he was left on my doorstep. He has a penchant too for diving into the kimonos of women and hunting for panties. Men he abhors, especially those who wear uniform trousers such as postmen, taxi-drivers, policemen and train-drivers. There are only two ways to effectively control him—one is stuff a large scent-bottle into his mouth, the more expensive the perfume the better, and this satisfactorily asphyxiates him for about fifteen minutes. The other methods is to clout him one with a stick, cudgel or hefty piece of timber.

At the station, as I had no scent-bottle with which to drug him, and, despite the morning chill, sweat was on my brow from the effort of holding together the suitcase of which he had already chewed a corner, I bought a pilgrim's staff with which to curb him, and I asked at the enquiry bureau if I could obtain a ticket for my dog. A student with symptoms of highly advanced syphilis in his face was the only one in attendance at the enquiry office and he seemed totally unable to grasp my enquiry in any language. Several old women had come up, with mountains of belongings on their backs, and stood wondering and praising the god-like fluency of my Japanese. I was holding Kumi up to illustrate my enquiry about a dog and the student put his hand out to pat him and was bitten. The old women informed me they had often taken animals with them on the trains and had never heard of dog-tickets. All I had to do was hold Kumi in my lap like a baby when the conductor came round.

'*Kawai des, né?*' 'Isn't he cute?' one of the old ladies cooed and the wretched dog promptly shot inside her kimono. The train came in and seriously upset at the possibility of my dog having contracted syphilis from the student, I grasped the staff, whacked Kumi and with a bow from the neck to the old ladies rushed to the train just in time. There was not another soul in my coach. There seemed merely a handful of desolate huddled figures in the whole enormously empty train. I tethered Kumi to the footrack of the other seat, growled and waved the staff to intimidate him into civilized conduct and overcome with Weltschmerz and the brain-bursting desolation of the early hour sank into liverish slumber.

When I came to, the coach was packed tight with human bodies and the racks were bulging with parcels wrapped in squares of cloth. My neighbour was quaffing *saké* and the two men opposite had their shoes off and their stockinged feet on our seat hemmed in my neighbour and myself. The people in the aisle all seemed drunk and were wearing rosettes so I guessed that they must be members of a works' outing— probably from an iron foundry if they could contrive to be drunk so early in the day. I saw some of them glancing curiously at my pilgrim's staff and regarding my venerable head out of the corners of their eyes—concluding I was a foreign priest no doubt, though I have often been startled to find myself taken in Japan for an American marine though never by American marines. The presence of teeth marks on my staff reminded me of Kumi but attached to the opposite seat's foot-rack was only a piece of gnawed leash next to a puddle. I put my hand down pretending to adjust my shoe but feeling under the seat my hand did not meet dog anywhere. How many stations we had stopped at I did not know, but by now Kumi could have found a new home or be on the way to a vivisectionist's table. Such was Karma, I told myself, both Kumi's and my own. I had to sleep sometime. I could not be held responsible for a dog's unauthorized gnawing of its lead. And remembering the long orgy of destruction which I had patiently suffered from Kumi, not to mention the severing of relations with the countless thousands of possible friends whom he had bitten, I schooled myself to bear his loss with fortitude. But he left a gap. The unaccustomed absence of worry about what mischief he was up to brought my nerves to a pitch of hysterical exhaustion. I remembered I was hungry and bought twenty yens worth of peanuts from a fat girl with a tray who was pushing her way through the jungle of people in the aisle. Fortunately as it turned out, I merely grunted absent-mindedly as I purchased my peanuts, for in the wake of the fat girl came an even more gigantic man—a sumo wrestler in civilian attire. He halted at our four seats and producing a ticket scratched his head and in a puzzled way announced to my neighbour that he had a ticket for seat 12A. That was my seat and my ticket had the number 12A written on it. The whole compartment was now interested in the proceedings and speculating who was going to dispossess the foreigner of his seat. I had given no sign of having understood a word of what was going on, but now the sumo wrestler speaking in very slow Japanese addressed me.

I threw up my hands in the best Neapolitan fashion and with a radiant smile firmly announced, '*Non capisce, signor.*'

The wrestler looked at me in awe. A fat little man was now encouraged and thrust forward out of the throng. 'Excuse me, but can I see your ticket?' he asked in excellent English, but looking totally blank and smiling warmly I discouraged the notion that I understood any English and the fat little man mimed what a ticket was and with fervent Italian cries of '*capisce! signor*' and '*al di la!*' I allowed slow comprehension to dawn in my face and produced the ticket.

To everybody's consternation the tickets both had the same number. The sumo wrestler stood dumb with amazement, deprived of his seat. Everybody watched him waiting to see what he would do. Would he dare to raise a sacrilegious hand against the foreign priest? I sat in meek benevolence trying to look as much like Pope Paul as possible, but ready to dot him one with my pastoral staff should he try by desperate force to capture the seat.

For two hours the sumo wrestler, and sumo wrestlers look like Tessie O'Shea's big sister, stood gazing baffled at the seat which eluded him. I gave him candid-eyed looks of Christian amity and sang absently '*Torno a Sorriento.*'

I wished I had had a pictoral cross to twiddle negligently under his nose.

At last the ticket-collectors could be heard bossily advancing and my sumo wrestler gave a furious cry like one of the higher primates whose instincts have been outraged and clawed his way towards the collectors who represented the Japan National Railways, the issuers of two tickets for a single seat. To pacify the indignant passenger, they offered him an unoccupied first-class seat and I saw him being respectfully escorted away.

At last I could go to the lavatory.

However, I had to pass the rest of the journey in that train in silence for I could not throw off my Italian mantle and betray a sudden familiarity with Japanese.

The two hours went by as we passed through vine-lands and then tea-growing country, and the compartment grew less crowded once the iron company's outing had got out. It was then that I noticed an inch of white tail protruding from the kimono of a refined Kyoto-looking lady in a seat by an opposite window. She was gazing out in seeming abstraction at the tea-bushes and I wondered if she was aware of her secret passenger. The pair of them seemed content and so I thought it best to let sleeping dogs lie till I had to leave the train.

Fortunately the pensive lady had to go to the toilet before the train came to my stop and with leash and seaweed biscuits in hand I threw myself at Kumi before he could get into another kimono. By growling and thumping him with the staff, I had him reasonably under control by the time we had to ascend by escalator to the level where the branch train would come. I suppose it is just his open-hearted curiosity and receptiveness to new experiences but Kumi's joyful salutation of every pole and corner and voluptuous caressing of all passing feet in a crowded station did prove singularly wearying, and I swung hefty cracks at him like a Zen master all the way along the platform while the Japanese gazed at us open-mouthed as if there were something odd about us. What that was I discovered as I found my new seat—my overcoat had split right down the back seam. What an indictment of modern British workman-ship when an overcoat falls apart, after a mere sixteen years!

I bought Kumi a tangerine to play with and myself a can of beer, but he wanted the can and glad to have him occupied I made do with the tangerine. A man on the other side began to take photographs of us. I smoothed out Kumi's ears so that we would look to advantage.

Outside were mountains of chemical waste. Gradually I

was lulled to sleep.

When I awoke we were passing through rice-growing plains, looking forlorn at this time of the year with gray stacks standing sombrely in the dying light. Kumi was being nursed in the arms of a young lady who had placed a small foam-rubber cushion under his head, and herself was listening to a transistor radio by means of an ear-plug.

'*Kawai des, mé?* Isn't he cute?' she said. I looked sheepishly proprietorial, and thought this was a propitious moment to find the dining car.

When I came back, Kumi was being fed silver balls of *jintan* and reviving cups of warm *saké* and having hot towels laid on his belly by the young lady who, it turned out, was a nurse. She apologized for her carelessness in letting the ear-plug of her transistor find its way into the intestines of my dog as this might bring about cancer. Kumi was starry-eyed and pacific under the doses of *saké* and so tranquilly we came to Yumi City.

CHAPTER FOUR

Tomoshige was waiting at the station for me with a small banner of welcome in his hand in case I failed to recognize him, or he me. He wore large thick- and black-rimmed spectacles, with his bushy hair well-brushed back, a subdued grey suit, a silk tie with a pearl stick-pin and a diamond ring on his finger. He was still the same boyish figure but there was just the hint of a faun-like paunch, which surprised me as much as the diamond for was he not a teacher of English? I had expected, despite his carefully posed photograph, to find him a little more emaciated and showing signs of pedagogic toil. But he had a confident relaxed grin and showed no obvious signs of having seven mouths to feed. Then I recollected that, as a Japanese teacher, he would have received a bonus this month and this would account for his unscholastic jollity.

As for myself, the sleeping during the day and having had only peanuts, a tangerine and a plate of rice eaten standing up in the swaying buffet car, plus the strain of remembering Kumi's existence, had made my stomach rather gravelly and I looked forward to a bath, a light digestible meal and bed in a Western-style hotel.

Kumi sank his teeth into the cloth of Tomoshige's trousers and as I was extracting his fangs Tomoshige held out the ring for my admiration. It had cost three hundred pounds but he had always wanted to wear a ring like a foreigner.

'Diamonds are vulgar,' I told him sternly.

Rather crestfallen, he led us out to his car—a Publica I noticed—and with reviving cheerfulness said, 'Come on, whack. Jump in.'

We had not driven far when he announced: 'Well, whackers. Here we are.'

In truth we had proceeded only a few metres along the broad main boulevard of Yuni City and circled into a maze of alleys that flashed with the signs of bars and cabarets. I had just time to register with myself a distinct surprise at Tomoshige's dreadful Liverpool accent. Wherever he had got it, it was not from me—at least I hoped not. I remembered that he had always had a precocious command of the type of idioms with which Japanese students are not familiar—but his proceeding to say, 'At the old Dicky Sam's' as we stopped in front of a bar struck me as unaccountable unless he had been researching deeply into Beatleology. The front of the bar was blushing bluely with a big blue and silver sign that read 'Bar Blue Camelia'—with 'FOREIGNERS ADORED' underneath. The blue and white door had burst open before the car-engine stopped and an honoring of hostesses in kimonos shot out with radiant cries of 'It's Tomi-san, mama!'

Mama herself, a trifle plump with firm white flesh and in a kimono of darker blue with lesser white floral dotifications to signify her seniority, was soon hugging my suitcase, while Kumi reversed on to his back had two dark-eyed charmers carrying him in. The mama-san's other arm supported my waist as with tenderness she escorted my self down the unexpected two steps into the Bar Blue Camelia.

'You've spelt "camellia" wrong,' I said pedantically passing the threshold.

'He's an intellectual. Oh I do so adore intellectuals,' cried mama-san in very refined tones. 'How do you do?'

'Mama-san,' said Tomoshige vibrantly. 'I want you to meet my old teacher. I owe everything to him. He saved me from suicide at the darkest time of my life when I was passing through spiritual crises. He gave me new values and new eyes. He taught me to appreciate nature and knows all about Zen Buddhism. He is an anonymous saint and for my sake, mama-san, please be like a mother to him alone in our land.'

'How old is he?' mama-san prudently asked. It turned out we were of the same age, and moreover both born under Taurus This meant, apparently, that we were both artistic and warm-hearted and rather impulsive in matters of love so that we were apt to be let down by the cold-hearted mercenary egoists not born under Taurus.

'Not that I'm Lesbian at all,' said mama-san who had con-

trived to give me a swift account of her life and informed me
that she was known as Midori, 'but when I say I've never been
able really to love a man—even my husband, but his sister
arranged that—I just mean that I find money more important,
don't you? I think it's an important aspect of our Taurus
nature.'

She had my right hand in her soft plump hands and was
reading my lines of life, love and money.

'It's most curious,' she said. 'Your money-line is terribly
faint but later on it becomes a deep strong groove. Have you
any wealthy relatives?'

'Not since the seventeenth century,' said I.

'Well, later on you're going to become fabulously rich.'

The film-rights, I thought, with an optimistic glow relaxing
me into the deep cushions and the nestling girls.

'It's the second half of your life that is most richly patterned
— money, success in love and a profound deepening of character.'

While my future was becoming rosier and rosier, a platter
of tastefully-arranged dried squid, processed seaweed and
caviar on pieces of toast had been set before us with glasses of
an iced beverage that I found warming. It proved to be
Scottish whisky, not one of the whiskies made in Japan. We had
settled into a great semi-circle of foam-rubbered deep-uphol-
stered seating around a small table. I was crushed against
mama-san who was exploring below my navel while three
young lasses quaffing gaily were pressing for notice on my left.
Tomoshige was out of sight under a bevy of damsels on Midori's
right. This is the normal mode of enjoyment for Japanese men
having a drink out, and in all the other semi-circular alcoves
one or two men had their half-dozen female charmers inflating
their male egos. A couple of oil-heaters were warming the air
and some men had removed their jackets. Kumi was in a sort of
alcove holding a flower-arrangement. He was vomiting with
éclat.

'Do you play golf?' Midori asked smilingly as she cuddled
closer and I observed the Egyptian medallion of precious stones
which hung in the parting of two white plump breasts powdered
like large New Year rice-cakes. She had been bedabbled with a

devilishly intoxicating perfume.

'I have always yearned for a set of English golf-clubs,' said Midori drooping her head on my shoulder. 'I think you are tired—all that long long journey. If you like to come and use my bathroom I would give you a soothing massage.'

I totted up in my head the price of a set of English clubs in yen and did not overlook the possibility of having to pay tax on them to the Japanese customs.

'Mama-san has a beautiful bathroom in her new house,' said one of the young ladies called Aoi. 'She has her own vibro-massage.'

'With rock from Mount Fuji on the rim,' said another girl admiringly.

European sailors at the terminus of their voyages find Japan a haven of voluptuous sensation, as indeed in the early days of my sojourn in the Japanese empire I did myself. But by now the thought of antics in the bathroom rather chilled me. If anything was to happen I preferred it to occur in a soft dry bed between sheets. I was tired of porpoising aquatic sports with a foot in boiling water while the rest of one froze damply and part of the body got grazed on the hard tiles or porous rocks which are inseparable from bathrooms. There are too many hard edges and rims for my comfort. Give me a good dry mattress. I am no longer a perfervid seventeen.

In any case I balked at a set of golf-clubs—I was prepared to adventure only a box of golf-balls on such an enterprise.

Midori must have recollected that she was dealing with a fellow-Taurean for she gave a little sigh and disdainfully let go of me and Aoi, who had a softer touch, took up where the mama-san had left off. With the heat from the whisky, the neighbouring bodies and the oil-stoves I had become sleepy and may have dozed off when I heard Tomoshige briskly exclaiming that it was time to depart. 'Sensei whacker, I've booked a nice room for you at the Hotel New Yumi—on the top floor of Yumi Tower so you can see as far as Korea on a clear day.'

Having a horror of heights I did not feel enthusiastic at the news but there was something in Tomoshige's tone that suggested he was about to bid me farewell.

'And where will you be?' I asked, supposing he would be

carrying on drinking elsewhere.

'I'll spend the night with my mistress,' he said modestly. 'I'll collect you at noon. I can't get away from the island so often so this is a chance.'

The girls who did not know English laughed gaily at this as 'chance' in Japan-English has the major meaning of 'erotic opportunity'. I wondered how my ex-pupil was managing to support a mistress on a headmaster's salary. Of course Japanese could perform miracles of economy. . . . Perhaps if I stopped taking a daily paper . . .

Kumi was finally rounded up from the toilet of the neighbouring beer-hall. (the Bar Blue Camelia did not itself possess a toilet and customers slipped across to the toilet of the adjacent beer-hall, sometimes never to return if alcohol had weakened their sense of direction).

The girls were all lined up to wave us off. Midori said somewhat tartly, 'Of course I would pay you for the set of golf-clubs.'

'I'll think about it,' said I.

'We'll talk further about it,' she said, thawing, 'on your way back. . . . They'd so improve my game.'

The glint of her Egyptian amulet was still dazzling my eyes as Tomoshige, an energetic driver, clashed his gears and skirting a soba-boy on a bicycle we kicked off to my hotel.

In the hotel while Kumi had been dragged off for the night to a basement which I had insisted must be of severe concrete, I had drawn the curtains to exclude the thought of the terrific drop if I should start sleep-walking out of the window. The air-conditioning made the atmosphere like a hot day in Fez. So I lay in the light gown provided by the hotel and opened the poems of Chiaro Davanzati which I had always found efficacious as bed-time reading when travelling. The only other reading was a large-printed Bible in English and Japanese provided by the hotel. I took alternate draughts of Joshua and Davanzati and was soon in the sound sleep of virtuous eld.

CHAPTER FIVE

I had been delighted to find a mouldering packet of Alka-Seltzer in the shop of the hotel-lobby as I had a premonition I would need something to pacify my innards. Tomoshige was a rough driver and on the way to the coast he had occasion several times to extract a little warm water from the radiator to dissolve my Alka-Seltzer tablets. He himself sipped ampoules of *Guron-san*, the standard remedy for amorous exhaustion, and Kumi licked an ornamental rock which he had filched from the hotel's fish-pool—perhaps in revenge for his night on the concrete.

The land was as flat as the fens and little flakes of snow were driven on the wind slanting from the Chinese mainland. I could only suppose the nightingales would either be hibernating or wintering at some Asiatic Riviera at this season. Tomoshige said it was much warmer on the island because of the volcano.

'Is it quiescent?' I asked cautiously, envisioning stepping out of bed into pools of boiling lava. He replied it was a noble sight and if I were interested he would direct the driver of the helicopter to fly us over the crater on the way across. This was the first I had heard of a helicopter and I became dumb.

At my age I am beyond shame. My neuroses are here for all the world to see. I do not have any fear of heights but if I look down from anywhere above the second storey I swoon, invariably. Those who insist on showing me wonderful views from the roofs of department stores, towers and lighthouses always have the job of carrying my limp body down. But I am not affected by aircraft. Could a helicopter be regarded as aircraft?

'How long shall we be in the helicopter?' I asked Tomoshige casually. It had looked an awful lot of sea on the map between the island and mainland.

'Oh, only ten minutes.'

'Are there no boats?' I asked as if indifferently after a long pause.

'Not in this weather. It would be certain destruction.'

'How strange to see cattle in the fields again!' I commented.

'That's not a cattle—it's a bear.'

'A bear—so far south? It's incredible.'

'It's the winter. Hunger drives them forth.'

'But don't they hibernate?'

'Not in these parts.'

I pondered. 'You did say a bear?'

'Yes, a boar,' said Tomoshige.

'Oh, a boar.'

I wish I had brought heavier underclothing. And it would have been desirable for me to have come better informed about the ways of bears or boars. There had been no trees for kilometres and the first six Japanese cypresses that came into view were stone dead, standing like knobby telegraph poles as desolate as the hags on the blasted heath.

'What happened to those trees?' I asked.

'Typhoon.'

I began to feel increasing sympathy for poor ex-Emperor Gogo. He would have had to do the journey not by Publica but in a sedan, probably with no decent road either.

'It's a good road,' I said looking for the positive.

'Yes, the old one went in the last major earthquake. Fortunately there's not much building in this region so there was little loss of life.'

There was utter desolation as far as I could see, except for wild birds, and I was not surprised as the place hardly invited settlement. There were old salt-workings from time to time. Far off there was the tower of a lighthouse and the slime-green of the sea visible over the line of a sea-wall. The sky-lined group of buildings growing larger as we sped up the road elevated above the salt-flats lessened the respite before the helicopter. The howl of the wind from the ocean and the ever more noticeable jumping of the ocean-surface, just like an over-heated pan of porridge, told even my untrained eye that a boat would be risky. I took hope from the thought that such weather would prevent helicopters from flying. Like the characters in the Noh plays we could take refuge for the night in a fisherman's hut. I was philosophical enough to linger here on the rim of the ocean forever. Of Nightingale Island there was no trace at all.

There were a few houses all huddled closely together as if for warmth. Beside one of the houses was a rusty hen-house but as I was noticing the lack of hens Tomoshige pointed out the rusty cabin as the helicopter. He was not joking either. The door, or gate, of the thing, I saw disbelievingly, was held on with string.

A cheerful looking man in white overalls with an oily spanner in his hand came out of the house.

'It's a nuisance that I can't have the car on the island,' said Tomoshige. 'There are no roads so I garage it here. We'll soon be across.'

It came to me that he meant to embark at once in the helicopter and I could not take it. Just looking at that boiling sea made me feel giddy.

'Couldn't we have a cup of tea somewhere?' I pleaded.

Tomoshige frowned. 'We want to get across while it is light.'

The darkness would conceal more, I thought. 'I do not like heights,' I said distinctly, but all Tomoshige responded was that the helicopter would not be going high. However, after introductions to his friend Shoji who ran the helicopter ferry we did go into Shoji's house for tea. Here I brought up the question of Kumi. Embarking with him in that helicopter seemed to me equal to certain death, but Shoji considered it a simple matter to confine Kumi to a small crate for the journey.

'Most dogs like the thrill of it,' said Shoji.

I dallied over that tea and my heart subsided and my head cleared. There was no further objection that I could make. I hoped to myself that I would not be the death of my companions, as persuading myself to calm and resolving to keep my eyes shut I walked to that antiquated helicopter as if going to execution.

Kumi was in a box behind our heads, whimpering piteously. I was wedged between Shoji at the controls and Tomoshige who on his right had that door insubstantially hooked with string. The helicopter itself was like a little plastic bubble and suddenly amid a deafening spray of sound we were soaring and the sea like a spitting angry face was beneath us. We were dancing up and down through the air as light as a sunbeam. The sensation was delightful.

Bits of cloud wavered past and we seemed like a petal to sink on the rug of cloud when the vapour opened and we looked at the angry corrugation of sea below. My head lurched and a sick frantic feeling of wanting to fall convulsed me, but by an effort I inhibited myself from moving in case I knocked either Shoji or Tomoshige into the ocean.

'For shame!' I told myself sternly. 'When American males older than yourself and female Russians are gadding about outer space every day, you cannot even hop over to Nightingale Island.'

'Here's the volcano,' cried Tomoshige. 'Sensei, sensei, look!'

I opened my eye a crack and saw beneath us a dirty big tellurian boil out of which steam was flocking and deep within at the bottom of a black shaft was a fierce orange glow. The whole thing looked remarkably obscene. Tomoshige had a look of religious ecstasy on his face but I was beyond comment at the time, strange delight of Japanese in such things as volcanos, octupus and bizarre-looking fish, Still, my response to the volcano was not so un-Japanese for I was fighting the impulse to throw myself into it from the helicopter even as Tomoshige was proudly narrating how many lovers committed suicide there annually. I had gone into a trauma and did not realize the helicopter had landed.

Even when I did, however much I tried I could not stand, for my sense of balance had gone. Tomoshige was looking worried but I told him it would come back in a bit. I hoped it would. In the meantime it was deliciously peaceful to lie upon Nightingale Island, solid earth, or at least so I hoped, for the volcano had unnerved me.

Tomoshige began to coax me with talk of wonderful hot scouse in the house and Kumi, who had revived, began to tear out my hair but no sense of balance returned to me. This had never happened to me before but I had never been up in a helicopter before. It seemed utterly ridiculous to me that everyone was vanishing into another dimension and their voices came to me from another world.

In the end a make-shift stretcher was sent up from the house and I was carried down with Kumi seated on top of me and penitently licking my face.

My old pupil Yuriko, looking much plumper and in vivacious health, greeted me with a worried look as I was carried into the living room and a space was cleared at the low quilted table so that I could lie on the tatami flooring with my feet reaching into the heated cavity let into the floor under the table. About a dozen neighbours, with white bands tied about their foreheads, were filling up the room, some watching television and others playing *hana* at the table. Cordial greetings were exchanged and everyone set about trying his particular remedy to bring me back from the horizontal.

Tomoshige tried the scouse (which was cold).

Yuriko thought whisky might do it.

The men thought massage of the neck and shoulders with sharp twists of the neck might bring me round. One of them heated my feet, and another put a flat hot plate on my stomach.

Yuriko's aunt, who was part of the household, remembered an old Shinto prayer and shaking a bough of berry tied with white paper she intoned the solemn words to drive out the plaguing spirit.

There was not actually a doctor on the island but there was a practitioner of acupuncture and—when all remedies had failed —it was decided to invite him tomorrow if I had not yet come round. I still could not raise my head without going dizzy and slumping back, but all the pummelling and the whisky and the scouse had made me feel lively in myself. With the help of a mirror skilfully dangled about the table I was able to join in the game of *hana*, a gambling game played with flower-cards.

No doubt all the men in the room had wives waiting for them at home. The *obaasah*, as the old aunt was called, perched in semi-invisibility near the entrance of the room, ready to emerge whenever a man wanted a match struck for his cigarette or needed slippers set outside when he had to go to the toilet. Yuriko, bowing humbly, would appear sometimes to creep around on her knees with a tray of tea for us or to enquire in a soft harmonious voice whether I needed anything.

The men were local fishermen. neighbours of Tomoshige. I had hitherto believed, misled by films and Kabuki, that fishermen spend their off-hours repairing nets. This is now out of date. Since nylon came in, fishermen devote their leisure to non-stop *hana* and poker. The gambling in that room seemed never to break up, for with the Japanese way of sleeping on the matted floor it was easy to roll out bedding for the sleepy while the keen gamblers went on all night with their feet tucked under the heated table.

I, however, was carried up to bed around midnight. I had the state apartment—a vast room with precious wood in the beams and an unusual scroll done in red ink in the *tokonoma*, where there was also a great fierce bronze horse from China.

I fell asleep to the roaring of the sea on the rocks below.

I did not, as it proved, have the acupuncture treatment though the practitioner of it was summoned the next morning before I woke up.

At about one p.m. I was violently aroused from rest by Kumi rushing through the open sliding screen and bringing a ton of military horse down on my head. When I was finally sorted out, my sense of balance had been restored, thanks to Kumi. I did not get up, however, as Obaasan said the weather was forbidding and so I donned a quilted jacket, ready to receive the household, and Obaasan lifted the lid of a lacquer bowl to show me the inevitable cold scouse. As I showed little enthusiasm, she brought me up the cold haggis which looked even more repulsive, like a chilled foetus. I took a deep Yoga-ish breath and in perfect Japanese said that I infinitely preferred a Japanese cuisine as long as I could have a cup of Ceylon tea with milk in it on arising. The haggis, I suggested, might go to Kumi as it had a suggestion of meat in it but Obaasan thought it would be more fitting to bury it in the garden as Obaasan had already spotted Kumi's enchanting habit of throwing up in gratitude at his host's or hostess's feet whatever he had previously obtained in the way of food.

My room now began to fill up with a couple of drunks, a rival game of gamblers, toddlers and the acupuncture expert, a fragile, transparent-skinned little fellow of about eighty in a faded dark-blue *haori* and *hakama* trousers. Though I was now beyond the need for acupuncture, Mr. Nigishi gave me a glowing account of its effect on health. There was a subsidiary form of treatment, I learnt, for the face to preserve immortal youth. Mr. Nigishi said actresses and some actors in Hong Kong and

Hollywood had made use of it. My interest died as I learnt that the treatment was not a hundred per cent effective but that in some cases the wrong nerve-ends could be damaged with Frankenstein effects. Mr. Nigishi also did a bit in the tattooing line.

Dispassionately considered, I cannot declare that I have a strong mind. I get carried away by the interests of the moment. I had always secretly felt a small tattoo would be chic—not a vulgar 'I love Elvis' but perhaps a small rose or a little black swan. In fact in Tokyo I had several times come near to being tattooed under the encouragement of men in the public baths. My fellow-bathers were all terrifically tattooed, with tigers, snakes, dragons and jungles of flowers, while I had nothing, but in Hiroshima where the public-baths are less colourful I was told that I must have been frequenting the baths of the Tokyo gangsters as only gangsters are tattooed. This had put me off though I was sure that those charming men who had scrubbed my back could not all have been gangsters. Gangsters have one major design on their backs, say a black tiger, and are not so totally embroidered that they appear to be wearing a skin-tight suit. Not that I wanted anything so extensive—just a little rose or, say, a tiny discreet black swan.

The upshot was that Mr. Nigishi sent off a boy to his house to bring back the pattern books and further equipment.

Those pattern books, from the Edo Period, were works of art in themselves and every page revealed new temptations of colour and form to me. I relinquished all thoughts of tiny roses and swans. There was one glorious design, in particular, an abstract swirl of pink, silver and blue with a central motif of a many-petalled lotus. I am the same way with wall-paper. Somebody should restrain me.

Not that I have any regrets.

Tomoshige returned at this time. Perhaps he is a little too easily influenced by any foreign example, but he wanted one too and settled for a line of wild ducks and a spray of plum-blossom. Yuriko never actually said anything to me but I am inclined to think she blamed me for her husband's choice. The wild ducks and plum-blossom are not in the same class as the lotus but they were Tomoshige's free choice.

CHAPTER SIX

It was almost a week before I went outside the house of the honey-bee. The weather had been poor and my wounds needed time to heal, for a masterpiece is achieved only after pain. Now that it had become a permanent part of me, I was not so sure that others would be so pleased with it; I myself would be less troubled with viewing it as it was out of sight on my back.

Nightingale Island has a gracious curving coast-line with a steep cliff on the south-east and south. The warm current embraces the island in this part and the vegetation is luxuriant. Wild camellias hung in flower down the cliffs and in places I spotted the banana-plant, though never a banana. Tomoshige to whom I turned for botanical information was totally unable to tell me if these banana-plants ever produced bananas. Perhaps the climate was wrong or they could have been male or female plants without mates. It is quite extraordinary, this inability of educated Japanese to tell one the name of common plants and fauna. Tomoshige was unable to recognize a sparrow and virtually the only plant he was definite about was rice. I resolved to read up about the banana and its sex-life in an encyclopaedia when I returned.

There were tracks but no roads on the island. Bicycles and horses were to be found but the usual mode of transport was walking.

The houses were of the same style as on the mainland, but set amid the luxuriant shrubs and trees the usual tile-roofed bungalows with their elevated verandah and sliding screens produced an especially agreeable sensation—like cool civilized temples in the wild greenness. One came across them with surprise as they were out of view till one was actually passing them.

I had thought that the famous seat where the ex-Emperor Gogo had sat in the blues and composed his collection of one-hundred-and-seventy-seven tanka regretting Kyoto would be of wood and commissioned from some rustic carpenter of the day. But His ex-Imperial Majesty had parked himself, it seemed on a large damp rock, without injury for he had lasted till the age of seventy-nine. The view of sunset from the ex-Emperor's seat was specially recommended, Tomoshige told me, and one day he intended to come and see it.

The ex-Emperor's tomb I found less impressive as it reminded me of a piece of wrought-iron sculpture in Leeds Art Gallery to which it bore a striking resemblance. If anything could justify poor old Gogo's laments from Kyoto, it is that tombstone for no Kyoto craftsman would have insulted him with such a poky piece of stonemanship. Tomoshige said he didn't think it mattered as the ex-Emperor was dead, but I silenced him with quotations from Sir Herbert Read, Sir Kenneth Clark and Roger Fry. Tomoshige said his girl-friend Murasaki was very fond of Sir Herbert Read.

I asked if Murasaki was her real name but Tomoshige said no—it was a professional name which she had adopted on entering the bar-life.

We had stopped in a grove, which I expertly surveyed and poked with an umbrella for adders, bears, boars, spiders and white ants before taking a seat on a log. The spiders in Japan are harmless but they are the size of cricket-balls and I have never become reconciled to their propinquity. The huge antennaed cockroaches, which are likewise immense, also un-nerve me but when you scream they go away, looking frightened, but the spiders do not. As Nightingale Island was so far away from the mainland, I was the more cautious as in the light of Darwin's theory I considered some more dangerous variations possible. However, all I spotted in the grove was an orchid, and Tomoshige unfolded to me his mistress's life.

Muraski had been disposed of at the age of eighteen in marriage to a wealthy play-boy saxophonist. He did not play the saxophone well—just 'Sakura, Sakura' in fact, which is about the same as playing 'Little Brown Jug'. But as he was so wealthy and had no occupation, he became one of an amateur trio who nightly toured the bars. He did not rise till the after-noon and immediately put in practice on his saxophone. The marriage (Tomoshige told me in a voice deepened with sympathetic emotion) had lasted only a week.

I was less ready with my sympathy. Muraski, it seemed to me, had acted with somewhat less than patience. But I was not going just then to express any criticism of the institution of marriage, arranged or otherwise, for I was aware that Tomoshige and Yuriko had had a stiff breeze earlier that day. The trembling of the horse in the alcove had roused me (my host and hostess coming to blows in the next room) and Tomoshige had a cut above his left eyebrow where he had come into contact with the base of a tea-bowl or flower-vase. It is my invariable policy when the guest of married couples in Japan to ignore all behind-the-scenes signs of marital stress, as I enjoy too much the comfort which comes my way from the polite fiction of the subjugation of Japanese womanhood. I like the fiction to be maintained in my presence. If Tomoshige had been wounded by a hurled tea-bowl, he should have counted himself lucky it was not a chopper. Apparently he had complained that there was a crease in his *obi* and Yuriko had upped with some ceramic object. Tomoshige had been giving deep sighs all the way to the ex-Emperor's tomb and I knew that given half a chance he would begin complaining about the nature of wives.

So I asked how old the saxophone-player had been and what were the other instruments in the trio. Tomoshige didn't know about the trio, but the saxophonist had been twenty-one.

'Just a child,' said I.

Tomoshige immediately accused me of siding with his mistress's ex-husband. After one week the brute had ordered Murasaki to get out and as soon as he could had obtained a divorce.

'He said she had no appreciation of his art,' complained Tomoshige indignantly. 'And of course being divorced she had no hope of marrying a respectable man—or anybody for that matter. So she had to take to the life of a hostess. She's so refined, it wounds her nature, but I try to spare her as much as possible and she's very grateful to me. I share her with the pitcher of the Yumi City Bats, as a matter of fact, but he's usually either in training or playing away so he doesn't interrupt us so much. He used to play the saxophone in the bath, too,—her husband I mean. I cannot understand,' said Tomoshige vibrantly, 'how there can be men who would behave so ignobly to a sensitive young wife who reads Sir Herbert Read on modern art.'

I thought it wise to make no comment on all this. A husband with money (it appeared to me) is entitled to play the saxophone, however badly, in his bath without objections from his wife, whatever her reading list. Especially in the first week. Though I would have said nothing yet Tomoshige asked me what I was thinking and to cover up an awkward gap of silence I said what was indeed crossing my mind, not for the first time since we had met in Yumi City: 'I wonder how you can manage it all—such a big family and the car, and Miss Muraski and going to bars, and then the house must have cost a fortune. I just don't know how you do it.'

'Ah Willoughby sensei, old whacker,' said Tomoshige in a voice of enthusiasm, as he looked rapturously at the ocean, 'I owe it all to you and Somerset Maugham. You were the morning star of my youth. Between you I was led out of the pit of doubt. I had lost my way in the desert and to my lips you set "the well of English undefiled" Who first said that?'

'Milton, I think.'

'English, you told me, is the key to the world's riches. And from the study of the wise and holy Maugham's works I learnt to be strong and throw away all false morality. I shall always rejoice I took English with you instead of Chinese with Professor Wong.'

Amid the floweriness, customary with Tomoshige whenever he gets going about the imaginary spiritual difficulties of his youth, I clutched the sense that he had been editing school-texts. Perhaps 'Excerpts from Maugham for Primary School Students'. The school-text industry is well-paid in Japan.

'Well, I'm glad you've struck a profitable vein,' I said.

'We're not greedy,' said Tomoshige complacently. 'Enough is enough. Who said that?'

'I'm sure I don't know. Some Roman, probably.'

'But I do expect to get the boys educated and through university from it.'

'The supply never dries up,' I said.

'No,' agreed Tomoshige, smiling.

'But you will need to look about for newer stuff,' I commented, thinking that by now everything of the late Somerset Maugham's must have been issued as school-texts. He is regarded as a great moral teacher by many Japanese.

'As long as it's Scottish,' said Tomoshige. 'What would you recommend?'

'There's Murdoch,' said I doubtfully. One is always hard put to it to name new British writers suitable for the youth of Japan. 'What age group do you cater for?'

'Oh all.'

'Well, Murdoch then. I can't think of any Scottish names except Maxwell. I don't understand why you are so keen on Scotland. And there's Mackenzie, of course.'

'Is Mackenzie as good as Old Parr?'

'I don't think I know Old Parr,' said I. I was not going to say straight out that I had never heard of any writer of that name—perhaps he was a minor dialect writer like Will Thom. 'Parr? Parr?'

'Like White Horse,' said Tomoshige impatiently.

My mind moved to White Fang, Jack London and Red Indians. I could not understand what a literate Red Indian had to do with Scotland.

'I'm at sea,' I said. 'What has White Horse to do with Scotland?'

'You've never heard of White Horse whisky?' Tomoshige asked. 'Where have you been living, whack?'

'But who's talking of whisky?'

'I am, of course,' said Tomoshige. 'You wanted to know how I make a living—and the answer is whisky.'

'You actually make whisky—here on Nightingale Island?'

'No, no. We don't make it,' and Tomoshige lowered his voice. 'We smuggle it.'

'You——But surely that's illegal?'

'What,' asked Tomoshige loftily, 'is law?'

CHAPTER SEVEN

As I did not on the spur of the moment know how to define law, I kept silent while Tomoshige went on with pride in his voice: 'We bring pleasure to thousands of innocent people who otherwise could not wet their whistles on the best Scotch. Who gave a mandate to those meddling Tokyo bureaucrats to command the average Japanese man that he could drink Japanese whisky, but not the best Scotch? The national contract, you tell me, but I defy you to bring me any historical evidence of such a contract. I trample on such Rousseauistic notions.

> Have I not reason to lament
> What man has made of man?

"Thou shalt not" is written over every bar, but with Prince Kropotkin I say "Thou shalt". Think of the battle to repeal the Corn Laws so that the Englishman could have bread at a just price. We are fighting so that the Japanese citizen can have good Scotch whisky at a fair price. Why should seventy-five percent on every bottle go to the Japanese Government? What have they ever done to deserve it—do they distil it, do they bring it overseas, do they spend hours pouring it out? By what right, human or divine, do they take it upon themselves to deprive free-born citizens of the heather-fragrant Scotch? There is not a sewer or a road on the island so why should we bow our heads to a ukase from a few officials in Tokyo? We are no longer under the Tokugawa but have rights protected by the United Nations. If the Tokyo oppressors forbid us to drink tea, are we to obey? Then why should we obey a clique who put Scotch whisky out of our reach? The essence of democracy . . .'

Tomoshige had won a silver cup and four tea-trays in the Mainichi News Oratorical Contests and he could go on indefinitely, with swelling intonation and Abraham Lincoln-like thrustings of his chin and dramatic liftings of his arms. He would, I mused, be able to make a truly impassioned address to the judge before sentence.

At the next dramatic pause I asked, 'Do you know how long you would be likely to get? The minimum penalty I mean.'

'We would never fall alive into the hands of the fascist clique's mercenaries,' Tomoshige responded. 'Though candidly I think we shall outlive the present evil system. History is on our side. As the world advances to knowledge, there will be less place for closed ports and tariff walls. I look calmly to the day when there will be a bottle of Japanese whisky and a bottle of Scotch whisky tax-free in every human household in the galaxy. Gladstone is with us,' he suddenly boomed forth, 'and Heine is on our side.'

'I think it's going to rain,' I said. 'I can feel my tattoo itching.'

Tomoshige said he was feeling peckish and so we decided to get under roof as quickly as possible. I was still staggered at the thought I was the ex-teacher and the present guest of an ideological smuggler. I might be free of legal responsibility, but could I not be held morally responsible to some extent for Tomoshige's development? I remembered a pile of old paperbacks which instead of throwing out I had passed on to him. There had been a copy of Prince Kropotkin's *Autobiography*.

Or had Tomoshige initially derived his anarchism from the works of the late Somerset Maugham? Old wine in the bottles of young heads. . . .

The Tokugawa had been right after all, I thought, in keeping out those dangerous Western books.

CHAPTER EIGHT

Obaasan began to knit me a scarf and finished it in three days. Very young and very old females in Japan find me a deserving object for knitted garments. While she started on a pair of gloves, I paraded the cliffs, gratefully swathed in the muffler, and observed the variegated volcanic strata of Nightingale Island. These layers are as colourful as the stripes in cakes and they have little air-holes in them. The effect is more like confectionery than rock.

Tomoshige, when he knew, gave me the Japanese names for different types of rock but none of the Japanese-English dictionaries which he had at the Honey-Bee were large or full enough to contain such terms. My efforts in the scientific line were thus still-born. It was the same with the sea-birds. Either Tonoshige did not know the name or if he did the word was not in any dictionary.

However, as we trotted along the cliffs, for I maintained the English custom of going for a daily walk even when gales were blowing (not from love of perambulation but simply to keep my bowels active in a household that stirred from bed only to group around the card-table day after day) I did learn something about the currents. There was the warm current which came close to the shore and kept the south-east and south of the island fertile, but further out were the swift and dangerous cold currents. The horizon was permanently misted. Ships went cautiously. The area has been noted for its wrecks in the heroic ages.

The lackeys of the fascist-imperialist clique, by which Tomoshige meant the Japanese Customs, were little given to patrolling this part of the coast because the currents were presumably considered to afford enough natural protection against smuggling. But they had failed to take into account such modern developments as Shoji's helicopter—if that could be counted as modern.

Tomoshige unfolded to me the recent developments in smuggling on the island rather as the managers of great industrial concerns give one a history of their firm. Of course there were no illustrated brochures, but the pride in the job was the same. All had started with Obaasan and Shoji deciding to find a new market for their fresh eggs on the passing foreign ships, and one thing had led to another.

I was not altogether surprised to find that Obaasan had been the guiding spirit in the smuggling. Shrewd old women are at the back of many great capitalist undertakings. When I recalled my own weakness in the air, I could only marvel at the intrepid spirit of enterprise in the old lady embarking on that ancient helicopter to cross the angry waves and find new markets for her eggs among the hairy barbarians. I bet she devoted a percentage of her profits to some Shinto deity of smuggling. But Tomoshige, belonging to the faithless modern generation, did not know the name of such a god when I asked him.

Tomoshige had several cameras and he put up with walking about the island mainly because of the opportunities it afforded to take shots of me looking profound or in action lighting my Chinese pipe in new places. Sometimes I was given instructions what to press and took him. We used a whole reel in taking shots of our tattoos. Obaasan, all the children and Kumi too were used as subjects. Tomoshige took several of me while asleep, and he liked to photograph me eating. This is just a national characteristic of the Japanese, not because I am especially photogenic. The better shots will be useful, though, for when my book *The Severing Wall* appears. There is a particularly fine photograph of me with my wrist-watch looking most elegant as I strike a match on a Japanese stone-lantern; it would make a splendid advertisement for Japanese cigarettes.

And so the time passed, with clicking shutters, till the day before Christmas Eve.

CHAPTER NINE

I had seen Tomoshige studying some papers—which turned out to have been lists of arriving British boats—but the first time I really knew something was in the wind was when Tomoshige and Yuriko both presented themselves at my bedside unusually early and bowed suspiciously low. Tomoshige opened up by asking if I would vacate the vast guest-room for the night before Christmas Eve—just for the one night. I could go back on Christmas Eve's morning. He was ashamed, humiliated and ready to spill his bowels at making such a request to his old mentor, but would I . . .

Yuriko followed up by saying that she and Obaasan would make me an overcoat of crepe silk lined with lime-green silk if I would do her and the household the service of taking the children out for the day—all six of them.

'But I don't know how to feed a baby!' I protested.

Yuriko said the eldest girl (herself six years old) would help me and it was quite simple really—all you had to do was put a rubber teat into the infant's mouth. Even Tomoshige had successfully accomplished this.

'Why—is Obaasan ill?' I enquired. But Obaasan, it seemed, was out gathering eggs and would be busy washing them. At this I twigged.

And I did need a new overcoat. A good one costs thirty pounds. Thirty pounds may seem a lot of money just for taking the kids out for the day but I may say I earned every penny of it. Unlike the parents of Japan, I do not dote upon infancy. I resent having to stand fifty miles in a bus while five year olds occupy double the number of seats for which they would have paid—if they paid, for in Japan seats are always offered to children while adults are expected to stand.

'Crepe silk would not withstand the rain. What about a nice mohair for the material?' I prudently bargained.

'Of course you must bring the children back safe and sound,' said Yuriko, having apprehensive intuitions.

'They're too young to know about keeping secrets,' Tomoshige explained, 'so the more they are kept out of the way the better—They're all washed and waiting downstairs.'

'What if it rains? What do I do then?'

'There are plenty of caves on the West side. Please, sensei!' I still looked doubtful, so Tomoshige added: 'And an astrakhan hat!'

'And the coat will have an astrakhan collar?' I asked Yuriko.

'Yes, yes, Willoughby sensei—if you go immediately.'

I may appear mercenary to some, but a Japanese baby, I here remind you, is carried strapped to the back, and the toddlers were two, three and four year olds so I had to carry them in turns in my arms. They showed great unwillingness to walk—spoilt brats. Those children were quite as difficult to manage as Kumi had ever been. However, even though I had been thrust out of the house at the unearthly hour of eleven a.m. when the rocks were not yet warmed, I had had the foresight to bring a packet of *chiri-kami* with me. These are the famous paper-handkerchiefs of Japan without which one goes nowhere. When the water-closet had not been invented in England the paper-handkerchief was in vigorous use in Japan —What a godsend they were now for the babies' noses, mouths and behinds! They proved efficacious also in removing the various toffeed products and the drips of the coloured ice-bags from my person, as well as the baby-food from the bottle which young master Five threw down the back of my shirt and in my eyes much as the squid emits a liquid drakness to de-mobilize its enemies.

I found it impossible to keep the six names distinct in my head, as readers of Russian novels complain about the difficulties of Dmitrovna and Pavelovski, and so I clarified matters by referring to the eldest, Hidemi, by name and giving the other five numerals.

I found I could keep Child Number Five, on my back, fairly quiet by exposing my tattoo for him to survey. The Japanese child is responsive early to colour and design. My method of pacification with the others was to stick something long-lasting and suckable in their mouths.

It occurred to me as I listened to the babel of Children Five, Four and Three that not enough research has yet been undertaken by our Departments of Linguistics into the early sounds made by children. The Jespersens and Zandvoorts make airy references to the first speech of children but do not seem to have produced detailed statistical evidence. The idea of my Thesis 'Proto-phonology: A Study in the Speech-Patterns of Japanese and Burmese Infants' which secured me a doctorate in linguistics from the new university of Runcorn was born on this outing. (I was fortunate enough to rope in a stray Burmese baby later). Subjects for these are not easy to come by, but this one was a snip. Any fool can eavesdrop on a pram. Having a Ph.D., of course, makes a difference of twenty-six pounds per month in one's salary in Japan—the difference between luxury and living.

Thus my first afternoon as a smugglers' assistant proved not unprofitable as I acquired an astrakhan cap and astrakhan-collared mohair overcoat in burnt caramel with a lining of light green silk (the lining being as important or more important than the outside in Japanese clothes)—total value thirty to thirty-five pounds—and indirectly I acquired a monthly rise of twenty-six pounds. To myself I vowed to work diligently at my new profession and prove not unworthy of the confidence reposed in me.

When I arrived back with the children rosy-faced and exhausted, it was to find the house empty except for Midori who was sorting out a pile of travel-bags in the main living room. All the card-players, my host and hostess and Obaasan were out in the darkness. With Midori's guidance the children were fed, bathed and put to bed upstairs. By the time all this was done, there was a fresh access of hostesses—all the staff, past and present, of The Bar Blue Camelia seemed to be putting in an appearance. The living room of The Honey-Bee resembled the back-stage of an old music-hall with females fixing their attire, snapping back their French-style silk garters and dabbing seductive perfume here and there. Midori asked me if I had done anything about obtaining her a set of British golf-clubs and on hearing I had been too busy to think about it abruptly removed her hand from my person. I could not help wondering why we needed a chorus of girls in our smuggling unless they were to act as cheer-leaders. Hoever, overcome with the exhaustion and emotions of the day, I fell asleep while lying on the *tatami* floor.

When I came to on a wave of heart-burn and apprehension lest I should have appendicitis on Nightingale Island, I heard weird English voices and, opening my eyes, saw peculiar English faces gaudy as setting suns. For a moment I felt in the hallucination of fever till the reality of the room established itself. It was true—there really were English devils in the room. I stared fascinated, terrified and repelled by the unaccustomed sight. For years I had not seen anybody English, except a fat English female professor one summer (who had looked like a mountain of meat) Apart from her there had been American marines who had their heads almost shaven, as it were, and looked 'lardy' and unhealthy. There is a blankness about American faces on all military countenances.

Anyway, suddenly seeing a roomful of English faces was unnerving. I had become accustomed to the neat Japanese face with its delicate lines and subdued olive complexion. These faces blazed. Instead of black hair these heads were red, golden, amber and brown—like the heads of chrysanthemums rather than human beings. The mischievous water-goblins called *kappa* alone have light-coloured hair in Japan, so there seemed something supernatural about these English sailors—and what pink or red faces they had! I understood how the Dutch and English must have appeared to the Japanese on their first outing to Japan. They had eyes as blue as flame. I was dazzled and stunned.

They were speaking some incomprehensible tongue in which gradually I began to distinguish words that were familiar; especially a fricative short word, that is not communicated to Japanese students of English, impressed me with its frequency. It was now obvious where Tomoshige had picked up his 'whacks' and nasalized pronounciation. The majority of the men in the room were from Liverpool; but the bald-headed chief engineer whose shoulders Midori was already massaging as she urged him to take a bath clearly hailed from Caledonia. On my addressing him in my impeccable teacher's English he looked puzzled for a bit and, as I could see his mind placing me as a Dutchman or a Frenchman, he said his home-town was Perth. . . . The Scotsman was not addressed as 'Baldy', an understandable mode of address for I had seldom seen a balder head as if it had never known hair, but was respectfully saluted as 'Chief'. Midori was whispering about St. Andrews golf-course and how much she yearned for a set of Scottish golf-clubs as she strove to strip him to his drawers. She succeeded in luring him with her to the bathroom.

The big living-room of The Honey-Bee was awhirl with Liverpool sailors and the kimonoed staff of The Bar Blue Camelia, with beer slopping everywhere. Japanese hostesses are lively enough with Japanese customers but with these foreign lads they seemed to think the Japanese refinements superficial, and intercourse was being sped to before my eyes. I was glad that no Lord Chamberlain was present and that the children were in bed. Of my hosts, Obaasan and the neighbours there was not a trace. I supposed they were busy de-bottling or de-kegging or doing something with the whisky somewhere. I thought that I should contribute to the success of the operation and I helpfully moved about the table pouring out peanuts for my sea-faring fellow-citizens to nibble. The girls, of course, were drinking the beer and then passing it from their mouths into the sailors'.

The television set was on, but nobody was looking at it. The sailors and the girls were mutually occupied and I was lost in amazement looking at my long-lost and re-discovered countrymen. Japanese have the firm unalterable faith that all non-Japanese have big backsides and tremendous penises, and they believe too that all Englishmen are gentlemen. None of these propositions seemed borne out by the evidence before me.

These English sailors looked like cheeky angels and spoke like fallen ones.

I noticed one rather lugubrious hollow-cheeked chap sitting by himself and catching my eye he informed me he was the steward of the officers' lounge on the good ship *Annie Laurie*. The steward spoke with a Liverpool accent as heavy as an onioned breath and came from Great Crosby. His name was Alfie Doyle. Alfie stood for Alphonsus.

'As soon as I see the Pier Head,' said Alfie, 'I say to myself, "Alfie, that was strictly the last. You will not go to sea again!" They're a rough lot, these buggers—all they think of are tarts and booze. Of course it's easy for them—they haven't the lounge to worry over. And the windows. Captain MacWhirter's very particular about the carpet. It's a Crossley—I can cope as far as Aden, but after Aden I come out with prickly heat. I always had a delicate skin—I just had to eat one mussel at Moreton as a boy and I'd come up in lumps. I'm always as sick as a dog from around the Red Sea to Hong Kong, and I've a floating kidney too. I'd never be cremated—my sleeping quarters on the *Annie Laurie* are like an iron furnace. Put me in the cool earth when my time's up. Mind you, they've behaved this trip. On the last run the Chief Mate was an Australian—some of them are very crude—and he brought a walloping big lump of blackberry pie into the lounge. A bit of the juice got on to the upholstery but fortunately the Crossley was unharmed. It was providential. The first thing the Captain does after his morning tea is to come and take a peek at the carpet. What with the radar and all that nowadays, they don't have so much to do. That's why I'm always relieved when Mrs. MacWhirter comes with him. She likes to do a bit of shopping out East, and she takes his attention from the lounge. You can joke with her—a proper sport. I've missed her this trip. Her kidney isn't too good either. Not that you'd ever notice, but she confides in me. You need someone to confide in on a ship, for your mates aren't really your mates,' said Alfie with intense bitterness. 'They'd steal the snot from your nose. I never bring a valuable thing with me and only my old socks, and they whip them, the rotten buggers. Dirty thieving sods!'

I had listened with respectful attention to this nautical experience, for I had read *Lord Jim* with classes and helped Japanese research students with numerous theses on 'Conrad and The Sea'.

Alfie gave me a detailed description of the Crossley carpet— he seemed obsessed with the subject, though I could not recollect any parallel situation in Conrad's account of the sea-faring life. As he grew less reserved, Alfie confided that he had a carbuncle on his shoulder and felt generally too run-down to indulge in any antics with the girls. In any case, he said, he liked to remain faithful to a young woman in Yokohama. She always came in her car to greet the *Annie Laurie* when it docked. He showed me her photograph.

By now the room had emptied of all couples except those who were too drunk or too impatient to reach the bedrooms. Midori and 'Chief' had not yet returned from the bathroom, and I wondered if they were still there or had moved to drier quarters. I found myself savagely irritated by Alfie, who was about to show me his carbuncle. Surprised, I became aware that my annoyance with Alfie came from my jealousy of Midori mucking about with a bald-headed Scotsman. I had not realized I was still capable of the emotion.

'Yes, it's terrible,' I heard myself perfunctorily saying about the carbuncle while my mind ran on whether I should burst into the bathroom and drag Midori out by the hair since her partner had none. Instead, I decided to get rid of Alfie and his wearying complaints. What did these pampered sailors on their holiday cruises in the sunshine know about grinding despair and misery? Let Alfie Doyle become an English teacher and he would have something to moan about. He could always collapse into a Seaman's Mission but there are no missions for English teachers on the face of the earth.

I begged the loan of a copy of *Sexus* by Henry Miller which he had brought with him to while away the time, and went upstairs to join the children in repose. I found I could not concentrate on the printed page or sink into sleep with the Henry Millerish tone of the household and the incessant to-ing and fro-ing in the bathroom. There are times when cleanliness is not next to godliness.

At four o'clock Obaasan, Tomoshige and Yuriko came into the room and crawled to bed, and I went out like a light. At half-past four all the alarm clocks in the house exploded and we had to rise to despatch the crew back to the *Annie Laurie* under cover of darkness. There are many inconveniences in a smuggler's life. The hours are distinctly irregular. Tomoshige's eyes were bloodshot, and my stomach felt as if ulcers were

imminent. Yuriko and Obaasan and the staff of The Bar Blue
Camelia seemed to be suffering from no ill-effects; they looked
quite placid and collected as they sped off the sailors in the
hushed darkness of pre-dawn. There is no doubt in my mind
that women have the natural advantage over men in this
business of smuggling as in so many other fields.

Midori without a hair of her coiffure out of place had
marshalled her hostesses as if they were a ballet-corps. Her last
tender words to the 'Chief' were: 'Remember the golf-clubs.'

The time was Christmas Eve. I could now (if one counts the
promised astrakhan-collared coat) consider myself a professional
qualified smuggler. The air was very cold. I was impatient
to have a sup of the beverage which we had smuggled and
which must be somewhere about the place. I hoped that after
all the strain and exertion of the night, we could now relax.

CHAPTER TEN

If any one time can be singled out in a country that remorse-lessly drinks all the time, then Christmas is the great time for drinking in Japan. The men have bonuses and the bars are packed. As I drank hot breakfast bean-paste soup and masti-cated my processed seaweed thoroughly Midori was briskly explaining that the Scottish whisky must be wafted to the bars of Yumi City in time for the evening. There was no time to be lost.

Through a chink in the wall (there are always chinks in Japanese houses so that there is both copious free ventilation and draughts galore in winter) I observed the morning star. It seemed to be shining in Midori's jet-black coiffure. I pointed out to her that the morning star was shining in her hair and that the ex-Emperor Gogo would have moulded a fine *haiku* out of the circumstance. She retorted that this was no time for *haiku*. The whisky had to be transported to the mainland, driven to Yumi City, distributed and watered in time for the bars opening at five o'clock. She, Tomoshige and Obaasan were making long lists of quick figures in their notebooks, while Yuriko was back to looking after the children. Hostesses were everywhere in the house, drawing on silk stockings, brushing their hair before mirrors and wandering half-clad in those funny sort of 'charm-caps' like dust-caps which Japanese ladies wear when in the bath. Even so, Japanese hospitable customs were not going to be forgotten and before half-past seven I found myself being taken to wave *sayonara* to the *Annie Laurie* departing to its Japanese port. The ship was too far out from the shore for our waving to be noted or for the usual coloured paper-ribbons of departure to be employed. The politeness lay in the thought. Midori at the head of the hostesses brought along Tomoshige's best camera which she had borrowed. It had a colour-film in ready for use.

The girls (I shall call them girls even if some were older than myself) looked attractive in the morning light as they tripped along the top of the cliffs. The wind blew back their kimonoes, revealing the inside patterns, and the long hanging sleeves flapped deliciously. Needless to say, being professional hostesses, they were all making sweet little virgin cries like a batch of convent school-girls as if to keep their hand in for the next lot of credulous businessmen, even though only the seagulls and myself were available just then for deception.

'It is like a Greek frieze,' I told myself.

Midori screamed. She went white and clutched herself. I thought we were in for one of those dramatic Japanese stomach-aches, which are no surprise to me considering the speed with which food is scoffed in Japan. Midori's eyes were turned aloft. She looked Strindbergian.

Swooping through the air was a helicopter, not the old battered thing of Shoji's (even my unpractised eye could spot the difference) but a brand-new shining presumably expensive model. There may have been a machine-gun pointing out of it, I am not sure, my imagination may well have added this touch from some harmless bit of tubing. Inside were two men in grim-looking goggles.

'It's the Japan Maritime Agency,' wailed Midori in a shriek that surpassed the roar of the waves.

Further along, nearer the house, Tomoshige and Obaasan would be rolling out the barrel, so to speak. Were all our efforts—my taking the children out and sitting up half the night talking to that dim carbuncular Alfie Doyle—to go for nothing? Were we to be caught with the contraband Scottish whisky and have it confiscated—and presumably drunk—by that impersonal and abstract entity the Japan Maritime Agency?

Midori thrust the camera into my hands as she hissed, 'Come on, dope!' and promptly—as fast as a lizard—threw off every stitch of clothing. Every one of the girls did the same.

Whether it was from the trembling of my hands or from some injunction from my unconscious mind I know not, but before I was aware I was working that camera. The women, a nacreous pink in the rather biting wind, did a folk-dance of

Nightingale Island around me on the top of the cliff. I had seen the folk-dance earlier, but it had been performed by men in clothes; as performed now, by women, without clothes, it did not look the same dance.

The performance was not one which would have been licensed for a Working Men's Club. It would, I think, have been regarded as rather fast for an English witches' sabbath.

A spell was cast on the helicopter for instead of proceeding it stopped, veered and came lower and lower. I do not flatter myself that they came lower because of my foreign face. Japanese men just cannot resist the sight of any naked females so long as they are not their wives.

If nowadays you go as a tourist to Nightingale Island, you may see the tree which has a lovely shrine at its base. I am not sure what species of tree it is as Tomoshige does not know what it is called—but it has acorns and the leaves are dark-green and not irregular like oak-leaves. The shrine is in honour of the God of Flight and was set up by Obaasan who looks after it diligently and brings daily fresh flowers and fruit. For here, by this tree the helicopter was brought down.

A remarkable sight. The two men were almost hanging out of the helicopter to watch the dance and suddenly the machine ran into the tree and dropped down like a ton of iron with a roaring jarring crunch. A spark flew from the ground. The men were thrown out and the messy metal mass of the former helicopter *BOUNCED*. This last bounce took it over the cliff into the sea below.

The Marine Agency men were unconscious. Midori hared off to alert those handling the whisky about what had occurred, while some of the hostesses tore up their undergowns to staunch the men's blood. One of them had a broken arm and suspecting that there might be other more serious injuries Aoi and I hurried to fetch stretchers and bring back some unsmuggled whisky as medicine for the injured Japanese Maritime Agency men.

CHAPTER ELEVEN

Everyone looked at me, then looked away.

All the faces of my former friends held an expression associated with St. Peter and Judas at certain moments of their careers. I had never expected my old pupil Tomoshige thus to disown me. Obaasan was looking straight ahead as if she had never heard of my existence. The very baby I had carried on my back crawled out of reach of my hand, and Yuriko took her child protectively to her bosom.

In the intense silence that made audible the passage of cock-roaches in the kitchen, I could feel everyone wishing me to hurry up and get on with my *seppuku* (or 'harakiri'). I had contaminated the household. The Japanese faces were unflinching and unyielding. *They* had all paid their rates and taxes; *they* were respectable and virtuous and were not going to be associated with the dirty foreign likes of me. Their disavowal of me was total, and silent.

The senior policeman snapped back the elastic of his note-book and said in a voice that he had clearly studied from English films, 'You must come along with me. And the possibly rabid dog also.'

Naturally the police had, in due course, arrived from the mainland. Sergeant Kobayashi seemed to be in charge. The tree was measured and the spot where the helicopter had dropped into the sea was surveyed. Further investigations were made on paper over cups of tea in the living-room of The Honey-Bee. The two injured men had been removed to a hospital on the mainland, and a report on the loss of the helicopter had to be submitted to distant authority. A Government agency naturally likes to know what has happened when a brand-new helicopter vanishes from the face of the earth. Ministers on such occasions are apt to suspect some private sale of public property. Everything was blamed on the tree. The helicopter-pilots would be charged with culpable negligence unless it could be shown that the tree had behaved in an erratic and un-treeable manner, or that an unexpected pocket of air had downed the helicopter.

The Japan Maritime Agency man who had not broken a leg made a statement when he regained consciousness. He alleged that the sight of a foreigner taking improper pictures of Japanese females had so shocked his highly refined sense of decency that he had blacked out.

The spotlight had turned on me and the first thing which the police wished to see on interviewing me was my aliens' registration card. Now such cards have on them in very small letters: 'This card must be taken everywhere with you in Japan and produced on demand by the proper authorities.' I was always so frightened of losing the card that I had never taken it with me on my rare travels, and so, of course, I did not have it with me now. This by itself was enough for me to be taken into custody.

But worse was to follow. Kumi sank his fangs into the foot of one of Sergeant Kobayashi's assistants. It was only a trivial bite and nowhere near a vein; Kumi was merely showing his doggy affection. But once the police knew that I was Kumi's master, they wanted to see his license. It was a frame, as I have never heard of any Japanese buying a license for his dog. But even more heinous was the fact that I had never had Kumi inoculated against the 'water-hating fever'—hydrophobia. This is a very complicated business and I was intending to spare a few mornings and do so in the Spring, but I could not deny that just at the time when Kumi penetrated the policeman's foot neither policeman nor Kumi were guaranteed proof against rabies.

On top of all this Sergeant Kobayashi was of the opinion that possible criminal charges could be laid against me for offences against public decency in that I did photograph with intent to publish and cause to expose themselves in a public place the bodies of Japanese matrons. The camera with its film was impounded. The film I may say was never returned and it is probably still doing the rounds being shown at police-parties in remote provinces.

CHAPTER TWELVE

I took with me only the early chapters of *The Severing Wall: Twenty Years In a Japanese Prison*. I was not allowed to bring my razor in case I attempted suicide, and tooth-brushes are thoughtfully provided in Japanese gaols. Kumi followed in another boat, being given respectful treatment as a possibly rabid dog.

I am often asked what were my reactions as, face towards the sunset, I left Nightingale Island for imprisonment. Naturally I was curious—who would not be? Going to a new school or into the army arouses anxious expectation. But stronger than all was my utter delight. Saint Paul, John Bunyan, Cervantes, Oscar Wilde and Brendan Behan—what illustrious forebears had followed the literary trail through clink before me! What a chance! Poor Henry James had never had such an opportunity. How much richer English—ay, and American—literature would have been if he could have only broadened his knowledge of life like O. Henry or Dostoevsky or Koestler or Genet with a few weeks in Wandsworth. Such opportunities are not given to all.

As the boat bore me like Prince Charlie, I began to write in my head the biographical details on the blurb . . . 'with his unrivalled first-hand experience of Oriental gaols. . . .'

I was wondering what photograph I would use on the jacket of *The Severing Wall* and whether a biographical detail like 'Willoughby's recreations are surfing and taming tigers' would sound credible when the very comfortable car which had carried me from the coast to Yumi City drew up at the castle-like gateway of Yumi City Gaol. The walls of the prison were sheer and quite tall; a guard with a gun sat in a little tower aloft and observed the car with interest. I fell in love with the place at once; there was a look of the Imperial Palace in Tokyo about it except that there was no moat with swans on.

Truly, it looked like an enchanted castle. From it I would extract the stuff of romance—my best-selling novel *The Severing Wall*. I could not be enrolled quickly enough.

Now, in retrospect, ripened by experience, I would like to offer a few constructive proposals. I do not want the governors of Japanese prisons to think that I am in any way criticizing what I shall always regard as the pleasantest and most inviting of prisons. I hope I shall hurt nobody's feelings by tentatively suggesting that hot-water bottles might be supplied during the winter to English inmates. It is little incidental comforts like these that make all the difference between the old wicked punishment and modern rehabilitation.

Apart from this, I have no complaints. The food and service were in every respect far superior to that in any Western-style hotel I had known in Japan. Every attempt otherwise was made to cater to my comfort and my least wish was gratified. The laundry service in particular was of a high quality and, of course, was completely free.

Because of overcrowding I was given de luxe quarters—the death-cell—though in fact nobody had been executed there from since the prison had been built. The post-war criminal code in Japan is extremely enlightened; murder for love and passion rates about eighteen months with good behaviour. You have to be a very vicious mass murderer or a slayer of children to warrant the death-penalty and even then if you feel intense enough about it you can go on disputing the verdict till either you or the witnesses die of old age.

There was no lock on my cell but there was (I was pleased to notice) a small bolt on the inside for when I desired privacy. I had been inside about five minutes and was busy arranging the flowers when there was a light knock and my warder came in loaded with parcels. These were from the Dayton, Ohio Ladies' Messengers of Goodwill To The Orphaned and Confined Everywhere Benevolent Organization. I still qualified for the Christmas handout and I shall always feel grateful to the sweet dears for brightening my first hours in my first cell. There were tins of beetroot, sweet corn and Maxwell's coffee as well as a big box of biscuits which I regret to say were of coffee-creams, a variety to which I am not partial, a box of

California dates and a plastic bag of prunes.

I was as pleased as punch. The name of Dayton Ohio, became stamped on my heart. Ladies, your little offering did not fall on stony soil—one of the elderly orphaned and confined in the world's grey wilderness shall always think of you as ministering angels and as soon as he receives the first royalties on the film-rights of *The Severing Wall* will come in person to thank you in your distant fair city. Those prunes were a god-send.

Apart from the benevolent ladies of Dayton, Ohio, I wish to thank the Governor (ex-baron Morito), all the staff especially Mr. Tatsuo Takohaobi (known affectionately to us all as Ta-chan) and, last but not least, the entire body of prisoners who all, in their various ways, helped to make my stay so thoroughly enjoyable that I shall ever regard Yumi City Gaol as my second home. I would be lacking in gratitude if I failed to mention the Reverend Nobuyuki Moriyama, the Buddhist chaplain, of the Tendai Sect, who kindly secured for me a portable television set and brought me many of those small comforts such as sweets, tobacco, fresh eggs, bean-paste cakes and flowers of the season which help to brighten the passing hours.

I have already mentioned the excellent laundry service, but the City Gaol has the good fortune to be built over a mineral hot spring of great curative power. The enlightened Governor, ex-Baron Morito, has had a fine bath built. Here the guests can daily spend happy hours recuperating their strength. The stones for the pools were personally selected by the Governor. Indeed one might designate the bath as one of the most luxurious and exclusive in Japan. I can personally vouch that when I finally left the prison there was not a blemish or boil on my whole body; my skin had a fine glowing tone as evidence of the hot spring's healing powers.

There was a large and very up-to-date printing shop in the prison and here all the examination papers for educational institutions in Yumi City were put through the press. As a result the prisoners could have made rings around any students I had known. They could discourse fluently about Wittgenstein, Bertrand Russell, Professor George Moore and Professor

Ayer. They would embarrass me with profound problems about epexegetic infinitives, ablatives and hypallages in the Old English poem 'Deor' and the personal name of the last Mogul emperor. Mind you, some of them had been professors and teachers in civilian life, so to speak, but even so the prevalent intellectual atmosphere would have done credit to Athens. The Governor (ex-Baron Morito) had translated the whole of Tasso into Japanese. His favourite composer was Mozart and he had lots of him piped to us in the cells and bath.

Meanwhile, enquiries were going on about me and I present verbatim the reply of the British authorities sent on by the Fourth Secretary of the British Embassy, some creature called Rhodes. I have never sung 'Land of Hope and Glory' since. Just because I never sent them a lousy Christmas card.

Honoured Sir,
As regards the person called Willoughby, he has not up to the present any *known* criminal record in *this* country, so far as can be ascertained.

Whether or not he is a British citizen is a matter that would have to be investigated once extradition proceedings were decided upon.

Talk about damning with faint praise! First they hinted that I had a sinister criminal past though I had not been found out, then they suggested I had probably been in—French, German and Spanish gaols galore. After this, they become sceptical of whether I am British at all. When taking my guineas for re-issuing my passport, they had never shown the least doubt. Then, to cap it all, they *introduce* the idea of extradition, which nobody had mentioned as yet, and down-grade me from 'Mr. Willoughby' to 'Willoughby'.

That letter is a good example of the modern decline of English comradeship. Lord Palmerston would have had the entire British navy bombarding Yumi City, while any American president would have already sent several stiff notes delivered personally by the American Ambassador looking very grave . . . I wondered if I should not be wise to follow Ronald Coleman and Auden and Isherwood to the States. . . . The Dayton,

Ohio, Ladies' Messengers of Goodwill might act as my sponsors. . . . Incredible though it sounds, no British consul ever appeared while I was taking the waters in Yumi Gaol.

I was cut. Just because I had not gone crawling to them with Christmas cards. I vowed to vote Liberal next time.

Though I seemed at the time to be abandoned both by my native country and the folk of Nightingale Island, yet, unknown to me, friends in Japan were busy outside working on my behalf. Innocence and virtue will always triumph over such forces of dark reaction as the Fourth Secretary of the British Embassy. I am not a religious man but no doubt my prison experiences were a necessary part of my spiritual development. Like King Lear I had to be tested. Unlike Oscar Wilde I did not become deeply Christian. In fact, with the Reverend Nobuyuki Moriyama about the place, I was dallying with becoming a convert to Tendai Buddhism. But I was touched; I was changed. Misfortune had an agreeable effect upon my personality. I was soothed, ennobled and gained a few kilograms in weight.

What I gained in confidence cannot be measured in kilograms. I perceived (with the spiritual insight born, as in Greek tragedy, from affliction) that I had lived like a poor blind little mouse, like a teacher of English in short, the slave of parents, school-authorities and the worst pupils.

In Yumi City Gaol I found the true lion-like Willoughby.

It was all due, really to the tattoo. . . .

The inmates of Yumi Prison were either not professional or not big-time operators in crime. The bulk of them were the type of bus-drivers who had been held guilty of culpable negligence in skidding and knocking down an old man of eighty-two; factory workers who had slain, skinned and roasted swans that had been classified as 'National Treasures'; minor embezzlers; one man who had posed as a doctor and stripped several young ladies; building contractors who had gone easy with the cement; traffic offenders who had tried to bribe officers of justice; professors who sold examination paper answers to college entrants; would-be members of parliament who had broken the electoral regulations against bribery; amateur burglars, pickpockets, pimps and peddlars of pornography. There was also one sailor who had got drunk and attempted to burn down the toilet of a bar. He had razed an entire district and, arson, being a heinous offence in a country of wooden houses, had received a sentence of eighteen years.

In short, they were small fry. There was not among the lot of them one really major crime.

Crimes of passions can be committed by any ordinary citizens, but the big jobs in Japan are the work of the gangs. These are somewhat feudal organizations with a hierarchy and are controlled by a boss like a feudal lord. You can usually spot a Japanese gangster by his having several fingers cut off (to cut off one's finger is an apologetic gesture among gangsters) and plenty of knife-cuts about his body. In my early days in Japan I had many interesting talks with young gangsters under the delusion that they were machinists with a high incidence of industrial accidents. Older gangsters speak in deep theatrical voices such as are otherwise heard only from actors in samurai films.

Now, members of a gang carry heavy tattooing on their bodies, the tattoo being the emblem of that gang. The tiger is one such motif and gangsters will take off their shirts to display the fine workmanship. The average Japanese citizen who pays his taxes will, of course, virtually pass out at the sight of the dread mark of a gangsters' tattoo. The gangs are noted for the sadistic savagery with which they despatch anyone who crosses their interests (that includes most prostitution, drugs, gambling and, quite often, civic politics).

Well, I had only to walk into the bath-house with my emblazoned epidermis before word was all over the prison that a great foreign gangster was in their midst. The 'boss' of the Lotus Gang no less, as a lotus shone among all the pink and silver swirlings. I moved on the plane of Al Capone and the president of the Syndicate. I had only to look at a fellow to have him trembling and giving profound ceremonial bows. The Governor himself expected me to precede him through the doorways. I began to roll a little in my walk with the correct Japanese gangster swagger. On the *tatami* mats I adopted the ceremonial sitting-posture of a feudal lord and looked with bitter impassivity while my inferior vassals cringed to please and placate me. It made their day if I allowed them to light my pipe.

When I made terrible blunders in Japanese my hearer apologized for his imperfect hearing and never blamed my clumsy speaking.

I had never been so fussed over since my grandmother used to wheel me around the lake in Sefton Park in my pram.

While I was undergoing this spiritual revolution and getting material for *The Severing Wall* in the City Gaol, Tomoshige was busy tracking down fellow former pupils of mine. Finally he turned up two of them—one running a pawnshop in Yanai and another a gas salesman in Fukuoka who were induced for twenty thousand yen each to write a glowing testimonial to my inspiring moral character at Tomoshige's dictation. Furthermore, Midori managed to persuade two Mormon missionaries, a Russian Orthodox priest and the head of a Trappist monastry to vouch for my hitherto unblemished character in return for her conversion to each of their creeds. The Reverend Nobuyuki Moriyama did a noble piece of brushwork on especial paper listing my virtues in Japanese.

This consensus of religious views about my virtue must have impressed the authorities. I had also, of course, submitted a letter of apology in which I put the whole blame for my not carrying my alien's registration card upon Mr. Rhodes, the Fourth Secretary of the British Embassy, and hinted that he was jealous of my speaking better Japanese than himself. As for the photographing nude females, I did not deny it but pointed out that the success of the Ladies' Basket-ball team in the Tokyo Olympics had so impressed me that I wished to improve the physique of English females by providing them with models of ideal form such as the young Japanese girl-athletes who had been training themselves for the Mexico Olympics when the unfortunate helicopter passed.

The Governor (ex-Baron Morito) presented me with a hanging scroll of his own making when I, reluctantly, had to leave. The warders all clubbed together to buy me a tie-pin and cuff-links of gold and black pearls, while the prisoners each brought their little offerings, humble but acceptable because of the devotion implied. There was not a dry eye in the place and the solemnity of the occasion was heightened by the snow which fell softly as in a Kabuki play on the scene of my expulsion into the grim world outside. The Governor himself held a large oil-paper umbrella over my head and escorted me to the limousine in which Tomoshige seated at the wheel had been waiting for me. Midori was in the back. The pair of them looked somewhat startled. For a start I was wearing *hakama* trousers and full Japanese costume (a gift from the laundry department) and I was speaking in the sonorous tones of a feudal lord-like gangster boss. Linguistically something of the Governor's aristocratic old Tokyo Japanese had rubbed off on me, and I had picked up a lot of underworld slang.

Kumi, by the way, was already in the car and fauned over me. He was completely transformed. I think it was the Japanese food; he had been fed continuously on dried peas and seaweed and it had taken the bounce out of him. He gave my feet weak little apologetic licks.

Midori wistfully enquired if I would like a good massage and bath at her house but I brusquely commanded Tomoshige to take me to the best photographer's in Yumi City. I wanted the *hakama* trousers in my photograph on the cover of *The Severing Wall*.

CHAPTER THIRTEEN

Since I wrote those last words, *The Severing Wall*, four fateful years have gone by and there have been many further changes.

After that letter sent on by Rhodes, the Fourth Secretary, my relations with the Embassy rapidly declined till I received a terse note from the Third Secretary, Forbes:

> Sir,
> In future communications, if any, with the Embassy, enclose a stamped self-addressed envelope.
>   Yours faithfully,
>   Augustus Forbes.

I wrote a letter to *The Times* pointing out the decline in the consular service and, a wise precaution, also sent a copy of the letter to the *New Statesman*. As a final protest, I relinquished British nationality and turned Japanese on the last day of the British tax year.

It was not a moment too soon for the sale of the film-rights of *The Severing Wall* would have bankrupted me if I had still been British. As it is, I am wondering, and my legal advisers are consulting with the International Court at The Hague, whether it may not be in my interests now to become a citizen of the U.S.A. or Peru. As an Asian, I cannot at present become a U.S.A. citizen unless some member of my family is already resident in the United States, and my Great-Aunt Agatha refuses to budge from Torquay. Peru is too high up for one who cannot stand heights, but I am told the sea-resorts are tolerable. Great-Aunt Agatha urges me to become Swiss, but I am put off by the Alps and the other Swiss. In any case the whole matter is still problematical as I have not actually paid any Japanese income tax; I am merely being far-sighted.

The English Inland Revenue people are still dunning me for

two pounds from the days when I was English and easy prey. I take a delight in dropping these demand-notes into the volcano of Nightingale Island.

Midori and I have a summer-villa on the Island nowadays. We like to get away from the smoke and din of the cabaret during the summer-heat. Midori has always been fond of water and she regards the ocean as one big bathroom. Both our children are aquatic. On naturalization I adopted Midori's surname which appropriately has the Chinese character for 'water' in it. Under her prompting I have also taken up golf. Ex-Baron Morito and the Yumi City Chief of Police are also keen golfers and we have many a pleasant afternoon together. (The Lotus Cabaret does not open till six in the evening.)

Of course, I have completely relinquished the teaching of English nowadays—I let my children speak pigeon, if they use English at all. A pity in a way after I had gone to all the trouble of writing that damn thesis on 'Proto-phonology: A Study In the Speech-Patterns of Japanese and Burmese Infants.' As a Ph.D. of the University of Runcorn, I would have minted an extra twenty-six pounds a month as an English teacher. Still, being a Ph.D. may come in useful one of these days.

It is not of the least use to me in my present capacity as head of the Lotus Gang (the notorious and much-feared Hasugumi) of Yumi City. In the centre of the bar-district I control the cabaret, the Grand Lotus, and on the second floor I have my gang headquarters and Midori and I our dwelling-quarters. We put all our eggs in one basket as more economical. The Bar Blue Camelia is no more (it hadn't a toilet and would have been condemned eventually) but the Cabaret Grand Lotus is very much in evidence. I wear a red silk dressing-gown and sometimes when I want to intimidate a visitor subtly, I let the dressing-gown slip a little from my shoulders to reveal a bit of my awesome tattoo. I think all the rackets in Yumi City by now are in my hands. I have control of all the pachinko parlours and the taxis. Recently I have been considering emerging as a public benefactor and endowing a new university. I would not allow English to be part of the curriculum. Instead there would be a Chair for Dante Studies.

Midori said she considered it would be a waste of money but

I pointed out to her that we must look ahead and if we had a university of our own, our children's higher education would be assured. I would like it to be a university with an emphasis on the practical side.

Another plan which I am turning over in my mind is the possibility of opening up the vast Chinese mainland to Scottish whisky, (smuggled whisky I mean). I have the offer of a good (if rather old-fashioned) submarine. The great obstacles to this dream of mine are Hong Kong, a deadly competitor, and the comparative lack of moneyed abundance among the Chinese population. Midori thinks we should begin by smuggling, *Japanese* whisky, first, to induce a taste for the drink. This suggestion is not without merit.

Tomoshige and Yuriko have had another four children. They are thriving, and everyone mentioned earlier in these pages, including Kumi and (unfortunately) Forbes and Rhodes of the British Embassy, are likewise. Kumi is now fat and lazy but still bites an occasional schoolboy.

Nowadays I am without a care in the world. Both the children are past their measles. Last summer I was troubled by an aching tooth but I had it replaced with a gold one.

In our flat above the cabaret we cannot have a garden but we have a nice collection of potted dwarf plants and a small wooden aviary of nightingales. On the island, I have the status of a genro, a revered elder statesman, and on the national level some groups, remembering Will Adams, have approached me to revive the Shogunate. But I consider that this would be more opportune at the close of the present Showa era.

Hardly a day passes without a telex from England offering me a life-peerage; The Queen, in a letter that must remain private, had dangled a dukedom and garter before me, not to mention various of her relatives. But I am far too attached to Midori and the children to contemplate a morganatic union.

Yet I have not altogether lost interest in these remote islands of Britain. As I sit, Tennyson-like, on some cape listening to the nightingales descanting over the breakers' roar, I contemplate acquiring a piece of the British press. This seems to be the only way in which one could stamp out the growing practice of following a preposition like 'between' with 'you and I'.

Bowl of Roses

CHAPTER ONE

I did not have enough money either to reach England or to return to Papua New Guinea, and in neither country had I any longer a place to live. I would have to stay here, trying to find new inner strengths, with only the calendar's view of a Yorkshire moorland stream to suggest coolness. The hair at the back of my neck was damp with sweat, and in the hot room the buds of the roses were opening as I watched.

Outside through the reed-blinds I could see the full September moon, but that made it all the more advisable not to go out for a walk. The streets would be packed with male groups ready to pounce once they saw my fair hair and blue eyes, just as a budgie escaped outdoors in England will be pecked and savaged to death by the native birds.

All around the city of Tehran the deserts with their walled enclosures were sombre in moonlight. The huge silver birds were taking off for East and West from Mehrabad Airport. On my table the first blood red petal fluttered down from a rose that had been furled a few hours ago.

This zenana life I found most wearisome. Shops and businesses opened from four to eight later in the day. At these times, women, with black *chadors* hiding their faces and bodies, and foreigners could safely venture out of the house. From noon to four o'clock all places were closed; the respectable population slept, and if one went out it was into streets scalded with sunshine and empty of all save a few vendors dozing over their wares.

At the end of the day, tired of reading in the weak electric light, I had opened the glass garden doors and curtains and was sitting in the dark watching the smudged quarter-moon through the reed-blinds. The silhouette of a cat moved along the top of the garden wall. All the jube-dogs in the neighbourhood had recently been killed by a squad of men with silencer-guns so there was no longer a clamour of snarls and barking as dogs searched the tins of refuse set at the roadside.

The cat moved gracefully into darkness and, as I stood on the small terrace behind the blinds, I heard the back-firing of a car some streets away—three or four explosions—then voices shouting, and the pounding of feet. All the streets around were dense with parked cars and entrance was prohibited from one side or the other, and sometimes both, so that in the confusion motorists not infrequently collided and there would be loud slanging-matches, the insults ferocious but no blows actually landing. I had no curiosity, at least not about these all too common altercations in the streets of Tehran—my mind was minimally preoccupied with the blur of the moon segmented by the slats of the blind. I thought I heard the plop of the cat as it landed on the garden-soil and in the darkness I imagined its back was rubbing against my leg. I drew back at the un-expected contact, and a flood of terror sprang from my heart as I knew that a trouser-leg had brushed against me, and the blackness before me with the warm smell of sweat was a tall man, pushing me back into the room. I sensed the tips of his beard on my forehead before I was aware that the light pressure on my chest was probably a gun. In a whirl he closed the glass-doors and curtains, and lost in the darkness with no sense of the room left, I heard the whine of my breathing and smelt the sweat soaked into clothes, endlessly, as if my existance had gone.

Then the buzzer from the outer gate rasped repeatedly in the darkness. Usually it made me start, but now it came muffled as in a dream, distanced by the violence of my heart. Then a light appeared in the small windows of the hall-door, and I heard footsteps on the stairs. Whoever was at the gate must have summoned the residents of the upper floor's flat. I heard the old lady grumbling as she came down the stairs, and the babies began crying. The metal outer door opened and her strong voice, dominating those of her son and sons-in-law, could be heard talking to someone outside.

The intruder whispered to me, but he spoke in Farsi and at first I did not understand. Then I caught the word 'door' and sensed what he wanted. Putting on the hall-light I opened

ne was and with me.

'Are you alone?' he asked me in Persian; this struck me as odd, but ignoring my answer he preceded to investigate the flat. There was another room which was empty and he looked in there.

'I do not speak English,' he said in English, and asked me in German if I spoke German. When I said a little he asked me if there was a back entrance to the flat, but I told him that over the wall, surmounted with a sheet of corrugated iron, was a neighbour's garden and no way out of it except through a house.

'I'll have to wait till the light,' he said. 'Would you please allow me to stay? I do not want to inconvenience you.' This was charmingly said after he had been an hour on my mattress, so I enquired with some feeling, 'What have you done?'

'I'm a student.' I did not look enlightened. 'Politics', he added.

I knew then we were really in trouble.

'The women from the top flat will be doing the washing and grinding cereals in the garden as soon as it's light,' I told him.

'There'll be a way.' He touched my hand and said, 'I'm sorry,' in recognition of my knowing the cost of his presence.

I explained that whether he stayed or not I would have to go out in the morning. (I had a class for 'Stylistics') and no one would come in, though paraffin-sellers, vendors and beggars would be sounding the buzzer all through the day.

'Have you anything to eat?' he asked, and I indicated the refrigerator in the hall and some jars and tins in the kitchen. There was no regular Iranian food as I didn't know how to cook it. He brought back from the kitchen a jar of pickled garlic, with bread and lettuce. I had always liked Chinese pickled garlic so when I saw that pickled garlic was a speciality of the Caspian Sea area I had managed to bring back a large jar, the others having spilt on the way. He now scoffed all the garlic, and the hall was filled with the pungent reek of vinegar. He took a carton of milk from the refrigerator, and squatting in the hall drained it, wiping his beard with a kleenex as at the conclusion of a satisfactory meal. Then he departed to the toilet. There had been no need for me to ask him to make

himself at home. I was only sorry I could not offer him a shower
—as usual the Swiss geyser was not functioning and, if it had,
a rush of hot water at this hour would have disturbed the people
in the flat above.

So there was nothing left except to settle down for the night.
The hall light was still on. I ignored his erection, which he was
not doing. He grinned, 'The garlic's putting you off.'

I felt enough had happened already that night without
my becoming an obliging rapee, and the pickled garlic was as
overpoweringly anti-aphrodisiacal as the prospect of stylistics
in the morning.

It was too hot to have a cover. He held my hand in his and
we fell asleep together.

CHAPTER TWO

His name, I learnt, was Feredun and he had studied in Germany and knew Italy and Turkey well. I boiled some water so that he was able to have a swab-down, and as I was about to leave he asked me to bring back a Farsi newspaper. There had been nothing on the radio news concerning whatever had happened last night.

In the street there was an air of importance, and as soon as I reached the corner I saw why. A car—a green Peykan—had swerved into a rain-gutter and the bonnet had knocked through and brought down the mud-brick wall of a garden. The wheels of the car, wind-screen wipers and all detachable parts had already been filched. Quite a stretch of the wall had come down and a hitherto unsuspected garden with a full line of washing was now revealed and a fat woman with her head veiled and buttocks prominent squatting and trying to look unconcerned as she ground a pestle into a mortar. Aged men chewing pistachio nuts and sunflower seeds and youths in flared trousers lounged in groups, all conscious of belonging to a quarter where there had been a happening. There was even a bashful-looking policeman standing behind a cart piled with melons and successfully disassociating himself from any connection with the vanished wheels and spare parts.

At Pahlavi Avenue, I waded out into the traffic and stood bawling out the destination I wanted till a *jitney*-cab going that way, stopped and added me to its passengers. My mind changed gears for the teaching and I forgot about my guest.

On returning, I queued for an hour in a supermarket to pay for a cooked chicken, a marrow and mutton. I wondered if I would find him gone when I got back. I remembered in time he wanted a Farsi newspaper.

To stay in the country I had given a written undertaking that I would not discuss politics. Even if I had not done so, I thought it impertinent for any foreigner, unless he had spent many years there, to pass judgments on a country's style of government. I was full of disquiet at the thought of the complications Feredun might have brought into my life. The torture inflicted by the secret police is notorious; all the more reason, of course, for my not having done a thing to raise an alarm. If I had found him gone that day it would have been easier.

He was sprawled in underpants on the mattress cracking pistachio nuts and was eager to know what food I had brought. The refrigerator had been cleared out. I gave him the newspaper and went to boil up the mutton and marrow with some lentils; I trusted the result would taste Iranian.

While I was cooking there was silence in the flat. We had spoken in low voices since the walls were thin, but he did not even appear in the kitchen. When I took the food in on a tray he was lying on his side, his arm over his face; his body rocked and it was an instant before I understood he was crying. Eventually I knelt beside him and asked what had happened. He did not answer at once, but indicated the newspaper and said, 'They shot—killed—Hossein.'

The young face in the newspaper was remote and unrevealing, an item from a passport or a police file. Feredun wept on for his friend. I could not read the newspaper account in the Persian script, and felt as helpless as when a beloved dog is dying. I left his food and began to eat mine while it was still hot. But talking was better for him, so I asked if the police would trace his connection with Hossein.

This brought him round to the practical present. He translated the newspaper paragraph for me and explained how he and Hossein with another friend, a student called Kamal, had occupied a flat under assumed names. The more he told me the more dismay I felt. The flat had been raided. Kamal had not been there, and Feredun returning to the flat had arrived just before the break-in and got away in the green Peykan, which had a false number plate.

'But they knew Hossein's name, and they'll trace his friends,' I said. 'And if they know about the flat, they'll have seen you.' Anyone who had once seen the bearded over six-foot Feredun could not fail to recognize him.

He joked: 'I'll borrow your razor.' But I didn't accept it as a joke and was surveying him to find out in what other way he might change his appearance. There were so many political prisoners; the secret police were everywhere.

'They'll get your fingerprints from the flat,' I said.

What hopeless revolutionaries these students were! Had they begun as if it were a game? I living openly was more secretive. I stared at Feredun as if he were already dead. He wiped his eyes with the back of his hand and sat up, and downed the stew with gusto.

I boiled a lot of water so that we could have a bath. To repair the geyser I would have to bring workmen in, but I didn't want the doors open so that anyone could walk in while Feredun was there. The next day, too, was the end of Ramazan, a time of rejoicing when Muslims begin eating again during the daylight hours so that there was a lot of bustle and noise from the family upstairs.

Feredun was in a state of erection, both amused and frustrated by it, and I was far from helpful, worrying more than he about what was likely to happen to him and also to myself. When a tyre exploded in the street I went pale, and at a noise in the hall I expected scrums of policemen to come in with the doors. It was only very gradually that I began to relax. Even if I had not been tense about the blocked geyser and political dangers, the surcharged state of Iranian males ever ready to be rapidly relieved in any human receptacle without a thank-you deterred me from the faintest flicker of Christian or human charity. But in the moony dimness of the room his fingers began stroking me at the back of my neck and down the spine, then his mouth kissed and bit, lightly at first. This lengthy play of fingers and mouth on skin and nervous centres soothed while it excited me. I was tranced by his delicacy to an ecstasy in which I served his strength.

I had thought that in solitude some spiritual insight might be opened to me, but by the removal of solitude he led me into paradise. Though I died tomorrow, I felt I had glimpsed immortality.

In the morning he shaved off his beard. He looked much younger and, with his smile and dimple visible, much happier. I felt both happy and serene, and there was a new relaxation between us. He joked that a friend of his in Germany used to say that a good dick is Allah. I thought to myself that, for me at least, this could be literal truth.

It was as if a sun had been hurled into my life, so that days must have rushed past without leaving a clear image of themselves. All the time the curtains were closed—the accustomed situation in Iran but not for me—and the Autumn sun glowed hotly on the curtains and the birds sang with fierce sweetness. On the way back to work I was in a fever of happiness, and snatches of gravely beautiful faces in the streets, old men leading donkeys, brightly patterned carpets being spread on the pavements are all that remain of those days. Of the classes I held I have scarcely a recollection.

Sometimes half out of sleep in the night or day I thought I was still beside Sari on the New Guinea mountainside. He was a slim coal black Western District man with a diamond-shape cut out of one ear and he taught me the best places to sleep where the cool wind blew away mosquitoes and how when something slithered nearby in the bush one threw a small stone. Then I would see the difference, the white face beside me on a pillow, and, lost, I wondered at the layers and layers of life.

Once, Sari, with whom I could communicate only in Pidgin English and at that not well, heard me speaking English. He sat enraptured and said, 'I love your mouth'. Feredun and I talked of many things; when he first went to Germany, for example, he did not have the language and 'walked about like a cow', as he expressed it. But when we were relaxed in conversation and I might have mentioned some totally unimportant thing like the price of Heinz Baked Beans at the supermarket he would declare '*Das ist eine private Sache*'. (that's a private matter) very seriously and decisively. This sentence of his always effectively stunned and silenced me. Everything I had ever said in life had been private; I was not a Queen at the State Opening of Parliament and Hansard-prone. I would ponder what I had said but I never did make out the force of this remark of his. In time I accepted it as an idiosyncratic expression of personality like Mr. Heath's 'That's what it's all about.'

There was nothing further in the newspapers. At work among my colleagues there was the same studied avoidance of anything which might be construed as political; one overheard gossip from and about the Court, a world as remote as Prince Genji's from the working lives of Tehranians stifled in traffic and bureaucracy, not to think of the many without work.

Between the house and work my mind ached over the political configuration of the country. The ruling regime was so firmly entrenched, backed by the armed forces and the U.S.A. with the former head of the C.I.A. as ambassador in Tehran. How could a handful of students—but were they only a hand-ful?—achieve anything with no popular support and power-base, but were they without? Every shop, office and dwelling was plastered with portraits of the Shah Aryamehr at some stage of his evolution, but what was the reality if there were so many political prisoners and young dead?

Feredun had a huge appetite—he liked all his main meals to start with a soup—and he ruefully complained that with the lack of exercise he was developing a belly.

'Don't you think,' I said, 'when it all dies down, if it does, the best course is for you to go abroad?' I considered, as I still do, that this would have been the wise thing to do, with him returning when events and new social developments brought him an advantage.

He loomed over me, his large beautiful eyes looking down, full of an amused loving pity for my cowardly prudence.

On the sixth day he asked me to telephone to a house where his friend Kamal, if safe, would be staying. My telephone was shared with the family upstairs who used it almost non-stop and would certainly listen-in to anyone speaking Farsi. Kamal might be in prison or already dead and, if so, the telephone at the house would be monitored by the secret police.

Feredun schooled me and at eleven in the morning when the people upstairs, all except the maid, were at work, school or the shops, I dialled the number Feredun had given me. He listened-in and signalled that he recognized Kamal's voice. I said slowly in English, as I had been directed, 'The parcel is arriving within an hour,' and repeated it before ringing off.

I had had Feredun's suit dry-cleaned, and he put on his dark glasses. He asked me to walk with him to the outer gate, but before I unlocked the hall-door he took me in his arms and pressing me to him kissed me on both cheeks. This was standard procedure for greeting or saying farewell to another male, but no other Iranian had done so to me. He had already thanked me before I telephoned. I could say nothing.

He walked briskly along the sunlit street without once looking back and vanished around the corner.

In the house I opened the curtains and the glass-doors. They had been closed for a week, and now the entering air stirred and trembled through the rooms and blew paper to the floor. The cries of vendors passing along the street sounded so loud.

I was again enormously alone.

His coming and departure left me completely disordered. I slumped helplessly on the couch till I roused myself to household tasks and became busied in an outer shell of activities. He had come and vanished like a dream only to sharpen my utter aloneness in Tehran. A shining hair swept in a corner of a room reminded me weeks later of his bodily reality. At night there was no one beside me in a state of sexual tumult. I wondered how he was managing—he had said he did not go with women, the prostitutes in the old fort, the only official brothel, being so risky and a settled existence of marriage difficult in his present circumstances.

At this time, with the nights plunging into sharp coldness, I caught a flu germ that was going around. I was less worried by the physical grogginess than the distortion of my mind. I seemed in a vivid malaria spinning through sun-burning days in Papua New Guinea, and I yearned with terrifying intensity for Feredun. Fortunately, an English girl returning to London wanted to sell her furniture. A week passed before I could collect it, but the re-arranging of the flat helped to steady me. I now had a bed, spare mattresses, a carpenter-made table, chairs and a small sideboard of polished wood on which I could set a bowl of flowers. Sometimes when I went in to a class that was not on the verge of a strike, the students would present me with a rose; after three such classes, one had enough for a flower-arrangement. Passengers in taxis and a young man in an electric-fittings shop had also bestowed roses on me, out of the blue in a free gift of beauty. At such times my heart stormed with adoration of Iran and its people. The only roses English men would send me, if ever, would be for my funeral.

My life would grow over Feredun, firm turf over a memory. It was better so.

CHAPTER THREE

The neighbours had trimmed their grape-vines and the chilly evening air had the rotting freshness of Autumn. As I put out the rubbish I saw a ghostly shell of moon, dead-white, above the flat roof of the house opposite. I was still feeble from flu, and even more so from boredom as the back-wall of the educational establishment where I worked had collapsed and the place had been closed for a fortnight to avoid mobbing from the extensive family of a student whose leg had been broken. However, I had lit my *baghtari*, a Persian stove with a wall-chimney and fed on paraffin, in some trepidation lest it exploded. The old lady above had come down especially to warn me as she expected the worst of foreigners. With the stove on, indoors was snug and warm and I retired early for the night.

About five in the morning the buzzer of the outer gate was pressed ruthlessly. 'Buzzer' does not convey the loudness of the discordance designed to bring on a coronary. I was threshing about in the dark to find a light-switch, then to find some clothes. I could hear the metal gate being beaten, and the people above stirring. When I opened the hall-door, the lock of which I had nearly jammed in my haste, I found myself facing one of the men from upstairs in a baggy pair of Turkish trousers and, at his side, a policeman. I know I whitened though somehow I refrained from dropping dead on the spot. When the darkness had passed from my eyes I noticed that the policeman was a mere stripling, an attractive looking beardless youth, and looming behind him was Feredun in a wild Cossack-type hat with other men behind him.

'*Mensch*,' cried Feredun, 'we thought you'd like to come to the Caspian.'

'At this hour?' I exclaimed frostily. 'And the policeman?'

'We want to miss the main traffic. He's here just to help. Put some warm clothes in a bag quickly. We'll have breakfast on the way.'

Well, it all seemed crazy. Feredun so happy and bursting with vitality and the policeman and the big stars sinking in the sky. But I stuffed some clothes and things in a bag, dressed myself for outdoors and followed them to the silent street. The policeman got behind the wheel of a Mercedes and I followed Feredun and another man into the back; we waved to my neighbour from upstairs, and off we hurtled along the avenues of Tehran, deserted except for street-cleaners.

Feredun introduced me to Kamal, sitting next to the driver, and mentioned he was the son of a general in the police. The police-driver was one of the general's domestics. 'We'll change cars at the general's,' said Feredun. 'We just used this for fetching you.'

I could not follow the set-up at all, but we stopped in the north-western suburbs before a house guarded by policemen who saluted docilely. The gates were opened to admit the car and while we waited for Kamal an elderly maid asked us to step into the house for breakfast and tea. The other member of the party, I now learnt, was called Nasir.

On the wall was a photograph of Kamal's father, covered with medals, standing before the Shah. The room was large and very informal, with neither traditional carpets and cushions, nor ornate Third Empire-type furniture and indoor fountain so usual in Tehran. Kamal's mother in a dressing-gown and curlers and the elderly maid fussed about food, and Kamal's younger sister peeped in nervously. When we went out again a sports car waited outside the gates and hampers of food and melons were being put in the boot. We drove off in this second car, a bright red one, and Kamal switched on some music. Dawn was breaking as we rushed along the highway to the north.

Herds of black goats were shocked to one side as we rushed on, over-taking any private cars already travelling on the mountain route over the Elborz and blowing the horn at huge lorries proceeding too stolidly for Kamal. In a country of wild drivers Kamal would have starred among the top ten. As the enclosed areas of greenery and scarlet pomegranates died out, the drop to the valleys below increased and the winding road overhung with rocks narrowed. At the worst turns there were mirrors fortunately, as Kamal scarcely reduced speed and the Persian dance-music throbbing above the engine-roar kept the eagles well away.

Feredun cramped in the back with me seemed to have fallen asleep with his hand inside my shirt. Nasir drew my attention to something—a cascade of water that was unusual on the desert side of the mountains. I noticed the hives of bees by the road-side waiting to be transported to the south where in the warmth they would resume making honey. When Nasir wound the window down to throw out nut-shells the oily bitter fragrance of wild lavender blew in.

Feredun woke up to eat an orange and at last I could ask him what had been happening. Neither of the other two had a word of German, though they both knew English, and so we could speak openly. All, it seemed, was well. Hossain had gone to a different university, and Feredun was confident that he himself was under no sort of surveillance. Kamal and Nasir did not favour violence in political opposition; they were student-friends, and Kamal had helped him. The third one, the other with Hossain and Feredun, must be the guiding spirit, I thought.

'Now that you're clear, for Heaven's sake don't get involved again,' I said from my heart.

Feredun was thinking of Hossain, I suppose, when he answered, 'People die for what they think worth fighting for.'

'But you can't fight for anything once you're dead, 'I said thinking of my cousin buried in Cyprus. 'It's not the right time. Your being kicked to death in a prison-camp won't achieve anything for anybody.'

He handed me an orange he had peeled and just said, 'You worry too much.'

At the speed we were going we were likely to be in eternity at any moment. When a car from the opposite direction almost grazed us Kamal yelled insults at the other driver who looked cowed. The Persian dictionary compiled by a lady professor, published by the University of Cambridge Press, contained none of the words when I later looked them up.

Mount Davidand was under snow, like a smaller Fuji-san. The air was so thin the ears pained. The mountains stunned with their stony desolation; I wondered if and how armies had ever passed this way in antiquity. Yet occasionally, far below, one glimpsed an opening to a secret valley. Did any small community survive there?

Suddenly we were over the top of the world, and the Caspian side came in a shock of water, grass and trees—denser as we descended into the looping valleys—juniper forests on white-rock mountains, and beech decaying above mountain torrents. Rangers in green and white uniforms warmed themselves by fires; they were there to prevent poaching of the fish. The cliffs and slopes of evergreens and autumn-fired trees became denser, and the warm cloying damp of the Caspian plain, with its rice and bamboo, enfolded us as we sank through the trailing mist. Feredun was sprawled across me, our bodies envined in the soporific cradle of the car. Lagoon-like, memory lapped me back to the groves of giant bamboos in Papua New Guinea, the silver-green pipes offering shade on the far rise. Here hedging the road was a smaller type of bamboo, and on the car-radio a programme from Russia, on the other side of the Caspian, came on strong.

Feredun had been born in this Caspian area but we did not visit his native village. (He had told me a complicated story about how he had been adopted by another branch of his family.) The market towns we went through all had a statue at the centre, and the buildings were of stone, architecturally more reminiscent of Russia and Europe than the rest of Iran. Outside the towns were 'villas', the bungalows built as second residences for the Tehran rich, and the thatched cottages of the rural workers, with pumpkins ripening under the eaves.

We drove by the sea, steely grey with snowy breakers under heavy clouds, and entered a town where the shops were stocked with stuffed birds. To my surprise we halted before the police-station. Kamal went in, and Feredun told me he had gone to get the keys to a villa used as a police guest-house. His father had formerly been chief of police here, and so everything would be laid on for us.

The guest-villa stood alone near the sea, with a huge glossy-leaved eucalyptus in front of it. A family lived in the lodge and the young parents and many children came out to carry our things, open the windows of the villa and light the samovar. Once they had left, my companions stripped to their underpants and fell upon the beds, for it was siesta-time and the early rising had exhausted them. Feredun made sure that the curtains were close fitting and locked the bedroom door from the inside, then slipped into my bed.

There were over a dozen beds in the large long room. The windows, screened against mosquitoes, had been opened when we came in, and the scent of wet sand was strong. I was pressed against the salt of his skin and sea-tangle of his chest's black hairs.

Time and death were the real voyeurs, not Kamal and Nasir. There are no women in the muslim Paradise, but I did not want such a Paradise beyond life and body. This was true paradise for which I had waited through my teens. He said, full of satisfaction, 'You love me.' His eyes were shining. I had said nothing. There had been no need for anything so roundabout as words.

We woke in total darkness, but Nasir had already got up and sent the young wife from the lodge into the town with money for bread and fish and so after a shower we sat down to a good meal in the dining-room. The bread was hot, the accompanying salad was made up of herbs in the Iranian way. The fish was without sauce and had been grilled with the scales on, but the white flesh underneath was fresh and delicious. In any case we were ravenous.

'What shall we do tonight?' Feredun asked happily. The stars over the Caspian were large and beautiful, so that I would have preferred to walk through the town along the shore. But young Iranian males with a car are as likely to put foot to earth as the sun to rise in the west. And so, changed and sharp with eau-de-cologne, we piled into the car and whizzed through the town, the glass eyes of stuffed birds in shop after shop flashing past.

Since Nasir and Kamal were healthy young males, the general intention of their finding some girls, seemed sensible enough to me who, from their glances, foresaw their joining Feredun in my bed if they did not. The streets were packed with roistering groups of Muslim males with never a female in sight, and the likelihood of finding a dance-hall, as Nasir and Kamal expected, seemed to me somewhat remote. But after half-an-hour's roaring along a deserted road outside the town I was proved wrong.

Out of the darkness rose a grand hotel, hideously modern, but from the dining-room came the repetitive lilt and beat of a real tribal dance melody. A group of musicians with sweat pouring down their faces were hard at it while in front of them men, women and children were throwing their buttocks from side to side in a frenzy. Some of the couples were in such a sexual ecstasy that the remoteness of the hotel from mosque and police-station became explicable. Perhaps someone on the roof was keeping a look-out for *mullahs*. I think Feredun paused for a half-second to order something, but then we were in among the swirl of eau-de-cologne, powder and sweat. There was also a whiff of pickled garlic, the Caspian area's speciality which I remembered Feredun wolfing at my house and was now reminded to buy while I was in the district.

Eventually Feredun and I dropped out and freshened up on the caviar and vodka which he had earlier ordered. It was the freshest caviar I had ever tasted. Nasir and Kamal gamely kept in the dance, hoping to get within pawing distance of one of the women, but there was more likelihood of finding life on the moon. For every woman dancing there were about ten males— husbands, brothers and brothers-in-law, and if Kamal or Nasir had touched a female buttock it was a reasonable cer-tainty that at least their hand would have been sliced off. A blue-eyed blond six-foot American was dancing away in the centre of ten circling moustachioed Iranians— a Peace Volun-teer, a fine body of men much appreciated in Persia. The tightness of his pants showed he was not C.I.A. despite the nearness of the Soviet frontier. He flashed me a smile, and Feredun's attention went his way. I was grateful for this as someone at the next table was goosing me and a quick glance revealed it was a middle-aged man, handsome and wealthy looking, but I left him with the impression that I was insensitive in that spot since I was not sure whether Feredun still carried a gun. I told myself not to drink too much of the vodka. Just then Feredun went to the toilet. When he came back, a number of men were seated at the table practising their English on me. Feredun was very polite; he insisted on buying drinks for the strangers, but when a new dance started up he led me off to the edge of the whirling mass, while disappointed and exhausted Nasir and Kamal sat down at the table with my would-be friends.

'You should be careful about talking to strangers,' Feredun told me in lofty disapproval, and I wisely did not protest that I had not initiated any talking. He did not seem convinced when, in response to his suggestion that I ask the American to spend the night with us, I said that the exchange of a smile and our being both foreign did not mean the American boy would agree to leaving his friends behind. I had scarcely uttered this in German when the American, dropping out of the dance to rest his legs, came across to me and in a few minutes, propped against a willing friend, confided the clouds and sunshine of his existence: he was staying at the hotel with four car-loads of Kurds. They had given him the solid silver bracelet with the turned-up ends that vaguely reminded me of something I had seen on horses.

Feredun wanted to know what had been said so I mentioned the bracelet and the suggestion that I help out with the Kurds, and, yes, I had asked Gary about him and Gary had responded he wanted another boy-friend like he wanted a hole in the head. Tomorrow, said Feredun, he would buy me a similar bracelet but twice the size, one for each wrist.

Finally, after midnight, the musicians flaked out. I suppose drugs had kept them going. Half the waiters had already gone and the remaining ones for an hour or so had been trying to get rid of the guests. Now the room and the hotel ebbed of life, and there was a vast night silence. We stood in the hushed lounge; there were only the two clerks at the desk. Stupefied with vodka we stumbled out to the car.

Neither Nasir nor Kamal mentioned a girl again—the hope was too forlorn—but they thought roulette might be going on somewhere. What I wanted was a good cup of tea. Roulette at this hour seemed to me a bit of fantasy. We drove along the front of the Caspian port; in the distance were white Soviet ships. Then I saw stone steps with little chairs, and heard flute-music.

'What's that?' I asked.

'For tea,' Feredun said.

'Let's have some.'

The water reflected the stars and the lights of the ships. We were about to sit down when a boy said there was a stove inside, so we trooped into a sort of little glass hut, all steamed up, where a lad was playing on the flute and another was doing a belly-dance while an audience of twenty or so men watched appreciatively. The dancer had a sweet merry face and the ripple of his body enchanted me, so obviously that Feredun and the others laughed at me. Possibly he was the local whore, but he could have been the god Krishna or Heliogabalus dancing on a shield. His remarks between dances set everybody roaring, but I did not understand what he said and Feredun did not translate. I imagined a Frankie Howerd sort of patter.

The hissing samovars in the small hut made the place hot and Kamal had begun to drowse. The dancer and the flute player were still going at full strength when we went into the revivingly cold starlight.

Nasir and Kamal were handsome enough—outstandingly so —but I would have preferred not to sleep with them. I had no objection to doing so, but it seemed superfluous when a relationship with one man satisfied me. Feredun, though, was carried to a pitch of joy by a multiplicity of bodies, and in any case, it would have gone against the whole code of Islamic friendship if Feredun and I had enjoyed ourselves while Nasir and Kamal, unable to satisfy each other, had stayed restless and apart in the very same room. To please him, I pleased them and unexpectedly, since they were vigorously gentle and gratefully loving they pleased me. Feredun glowed with pride at my versatility, just as he would have sulked and become angry if I had been unresponsive to his friends, or been madly offended if I had appeared to smile at a stranger.

As a result of all this erotic activity, my three companions were clear of eye and eating enormous meals, while the week on the Caspian coast passed for me as a sort of dream shot with excursions to the sunny blue daylight.

On the way to the sea-front we would pass groups of Russians from the ships. Feredun said that the Iranian secret police kept anyone who talked with them under surveillance. Most of the programmes on the radio were from Russia, a fare of un-inspiring *muzak*. We would hire a boat with a boatman and enjoy the sea and sun, returning to the coast for a meal at some isolated little fish-restaurant.

On other days we drove through the mountains to remote villages like Kharkol where the villagers told us that in the winter wolves came into the main street. The day before we returned to Teheran we collected lots of autumnal beech sprays to take back with us, as well as a good supply of pickled garlic.

A light snow had fallen and we had not reached the crest of the mountains when a crescent moon began to glitter. The last waterfall we passed on the Caspian side had frozen, and the road surface was dangerous with ice. One of the jars of pickled garlic had a leaking lid and though we ate the garlic and threw out the jar and vinegar the interior of the car remained pungent.

Kamal (for a wonder) drove with care. The radio for some reason failed to blare and the old Persian music had a pleasant quiet melancholy. The car was like a little bubble of humanity amid the freezing white immensity where a skid would have brought agonizing death. I was frightened of the lonely black drop on my side of the car, but Feredun was with me. I didn't want the holiday ever to end.

CHAPTER FOUR

At the college I discovered that while I was out of Teheran the other teachers had had their pay doubled, but I, who had not complained in energetic Iranian fashion, was left at the old rate. The college had also been nationalized and a course in phonetics had been allotted to me in addition to the other work. I merely shrugged as this situation left me free to leave when it was convenient for me. If I had not been fascinated by Feredun—and through him and because of him in love with the minutiae of Persian life—I would have taken the chance which had offered itself to fly to a job in Kenya.

I had just settled into the flat again when the winter arrived in strength with thunderstorms and long downpours. I had lit the paraffin stove, which adequately heated the whole place, and made the flat as pleasant as possible with vases of white chrysanthemums and mirrors. Feredun had not bought me the gold bracelet but he had given me an Iranian woollen hat with matching gloves, so I was equipped for the outside cold. He had also given me lots of telephone numbers so that I could contact him at almost any time, and he was rather hurt that I never used them. But since he called at the flat nearly every day nothing was left over for telephone conversations.

Whenever I was in the house, the buzzer was likely to go with its loudness always making me start in terror. Feredun or Nasir or Kamal would be at the outer door, singly or together, and usually ravenous. Often they would take me to a restaurant, or they would improvise a meal from what was in the refrigerator. The other pressers of the bell were the *naft*-men, the sellers of paraffin.

Nearly all households in Teheran use *naft* for heating and cooking. The previous winter I had gone into the streets and found one of the men who push little carts stacked with drums of paraffin. During the summer-heat he had ceased coming.

Now I had located a new source of paraffin, a handsome young man who surprised me by charging only the official price, speaking English and invoking the blessings of Allah upon me. But unaccountably a third man, with a little weasel face and his paraffin-drums on a motorized wagon, also turned up every day with long deafening buzzing, and the previous winter's man reappeared. When I was in the house there was scarcely a minute's peace with the three *naft*-men crying for my custom, and Feredun and his vying friends wanted my company. Finally I wedged a piece of foam-rubber near the buzzer, and I had spare keys for the outer and inner doors made for Feredun.

My sudden change to a social life did not go unnoticed by the people in the upper flat; the old lady in particular was impressed by Feredun's appearance and personality and liked to come into the hall whenever he appeared and have a conversation, as she did also when he telephoned.

'She says she thinks of me like her son,' said Feredun rather smugly.

I was a bit irritated by this monopolizing of my boy-friend and wondered to myself how the old girl would have reacted if she had known of his first appearance in the building with a gun in his pocket.

One evening, having returned exhausted at seven, I was lying flat on the floor when the key grated in the lock and Feredun put his head in to command, 'Hurry up. We're going out in the car.' He was always in a rush and on such occasions I hardly knew what clothes I put on. But tonight I was glad of the company, for my head was ringing from the row I had had with Seied-of, one of the students. Iranian students go through almost non-stop exams, and they have the right to demand a re-marking of every paper. Because of this I always read the papers with great care and gave the highest marks I possibly could, since a failed student simply re-sits the examination over and over again till he does pass. Fat moony-faced Seied-of had hardly any English and was not very bright. Recently he had found favour with the administration-staff and saw the chance of making an upwards alteration in his old grades. He decided to pressure me but as he had not enough

English to do so himself he had brought along a friend, an old hand at insulting foreign teachers. At first I had been wary; I try not to be beguiled into any discussion about marks, but I was trapped into saying, 'Not even for a diamond bracelet.'

'I cannot offer you a diamond bracelet,' said Seied-of in his slow English, very seriously.

'You are not God,' put in his friend pugnaciously. 'Probably you didn't read his paper. You should try to help him.' Seied-of lowered his eyes and tried to look innocently helpless, while his friend spoke warmly about the injustices done by the English in Persia and everywhere else since their first coming, and I countered with my usual gambits such as clutching my heart and falling back in a faint or raising my hands to Heaven as the only source of justice or referring to some regulation, real or imaginary, of the Ministry of Education. Seied-of listened, fascinated, to the clash of insult between me and his benefactor. I managed to terminate the discussion only with reference to His Royal Highness Prince Charles who did not have his marks raised, when he was a student, just because he was Prince Charles. But this made a feeble impression as the Crown Prince of Iran's teachers were always dismissed when he got low marks. The central heating in the college either did not work or came on as hot as hell and during the dispute it came on so hot and strong that, bathed in sweat, I nearly did faint away in reality.

Bursting with vitality, Feredun was not aware of these my tribulations and with my shoes unlaced I was hustled out to the car where Kamal sat at the wheel with Nasir by his side, both looking rosy-faced while the windscreen-wiper methodically removed the moist snowflakes. The car shot forward; after a while I understood we were going to the south of the city.

Feredun asked me if I liked *taryak*. I avoided even the slightest pain-killers whenever possible so, of course, I had no acquaintance with opium.

'Sometimes it's good,' Feredun commented. 'Do you want to try?'

'Just a bit.'

Soon it was evident that they had as yet no supply, for the car turned and nosed into mazes of alleys or *kuchés* where a man with a bright-coloured bellyband or an old woman would come out of the shadows and give further directions. The cold weather had caused an increased demand for the drug, which is grown in Iran and widely used for everything from toothache to pacifying babies, but except for licensed users, it is, in theory, forbidden.

We were in a part of Teheran where, if I had been on my own, I would have been knifed or knocked unconscious with a brick, my pockets cleaned out and my clothing sold within ten minutes of being stripped off me. But in the fish-tank of the car a small blue-eyed foreigner was safe, doubly so when flanked by Feredun who had said he would knock out the teeth of anyone molesting me. At night, with the snow gentle over all, the brick houses, walls and alleys looked attractive enough—no worse than Liverpool or Osaka—but the men had a sinister shiftiness and were ready to evaporate if a car contained police or military.

In the course of all this stopping, entering alleys and back-tracking we picked up a new passenger, a young man who I assumed was a friend of the others and realized only later had been unknown till headlights revealed his existence. The districts were becoming sleazier—dark alleys lit with a dim electric bulb instead of the gas-lamps of Jack the Ripper's Whitechapel—when the new arrival returned to the car with a triumphant look, and we headed to the centre of the city again. We stopped once—the young man going into an all-night chemist's shop and returning with a bag of sweets. The car went along Pahlavi Avenue past the Marble Palace and turned and stopped in a side-street before an old block of flats. Our destination was the top-flat.

The hall of the flat was very large and from the number of rolled-up mattresses a lot of people must have been using it as a bedroom. But what made me pause (till Feredun nudged me on) were the several cages of budgerigars and the seeds spilled from the cages and not swept up.

In the main room, that had a Picasso mural, young men were reclining on Persian cushions and talking. Tea was made and while being distributed charcoal was set on a square of wire mesh on top of the Aladdin heater.

The guide now became the guardian of the charcoal and

opium, which resembled a piece of yeast off which a scrap was rolled into a tiny pellet and heated, till it bubbled in the bowl of a pipe. I was the first to be handed the pipe, and as I was ignorant of its use I was instructed how to suck in and to keep the pellet hot. Nothing dramatic happened; later I was aware that minor pains in my knuckles and legs had gone, but this was the only effect on me. After I had smoked four pellets the pipe was cleared and re-fuelled and passed on. Relaxing, some of the men opened their flies. The conversation flowed slowly. After many pipes, the guardian opened a window and drove out the smell of the smoke. Feredun pulled me down to use his belly as a pillow, one hand playing with my hair.

I didn't understand what they were talking about but it sounded peaceful.

It was like hearing sounds from under the surface of a crystal pool.

During the first snow I visited the flat where Feredun, Nasir and Kamal lived. It was below Shah Reza Avenue and had its own ground floor entrance at a side of the building not over-looked by the flats above. Kamal lived there to be away from the restrictions of his family, I supposed at first.

What surprised me on entering were the many beautiful and expensive old carpets. Since teachers are so poorly paid, I had forgotten that in the Middle East, students can be accustomed to wealth.

The same evening I met their landlord, who came from his own house some streets away. Esmail was about forty, a handsome distinguished-looking man who spoke several languages and was a great talker. I thought he must be a professor, but it turned out that earlier in life had had been a mullah. His interest in politics had not exactly led him from Islam but to that curious synthesis of Mohammedism and Marxism which the Shah's regime was trying to destroy.

That evening everything fell into place. Esmail was the political guru of the three younger men. I wondered how Feredun could have been so naive as to fall under the spell, for he had some knowledge of Europe and he lacked mahometan fanaticism, but from the narrowness of his early life, I did not know though I guessed his need for companionship and love.

Kamal's attitude dismayed me; with his well-to-do background I instinctively felt that his politics were superficial but a remark of his, uttered in anger, dumbfounded me with its ringing suicidal immaturity: 'We will die for it.' Hossein was already dead for Islamic Marxism, and the Shah had plenty more bullets, and the political prisons were numerous. To die in Iran was only too easy. To overthrow and build demanded, it seemed to me, a strategy of living, of wily waiting for the enemy's moment of weakness. I hated Esmail for the easy fluency with which he would despatch young men, only too credulous and willing, to early death.

Yet, apart from my contribution which so angered Kamal that he burst out with, 'We will die for it,' I said nothing. This was not my country, and what foreigner could say whether Esmail was wrong or right? Probably his whole life had been a pursuit of truth leading to the point when he was pitted against the ruling family in a country where no opposition was permitted. But to throw oneself on bayonets—I saw futility and they nobility.

I sensed that there was something afoot.

When Esmail left, I was not able to relax—I did not know whether I had cowardice or a better sense of political timing, but I had a strong misgiving that this little group was foolhardy. The secret police quite likely had the house under observation at that moment.

Feredun was aware of my gloom; he sensed my very thoughts and was not deceived by my façade, now or at other times, this being the most annoying thing about our relationship, and before we were even in bed he made clear that my intelligence and political understanding were not the assets he most valued about me.

CHAPTER FIVE

At least once an hour the American forces' radio belted out '*O Tannenbaum*' in honour of Christmas—the tune stirring up a sediment of the British Labour Party's socialism—and spruces were for sale at some street corners in my largely Armenian district. The weather kept swinging from bright hot sunshine in the afternoons to heavy snowstorms. A water shortage had been announced, but the inhabitants of Teheran continued to hose the pavements with fresh water and sometimes in the mornings I managed to cross the mirrors of ice only by going on all-fours.

On a cold bright morning Feredun turned up unexpectedly in a new car, which I was expected to enthuse over though I seldom saw much difference between one and another except the colour. This one had a lever near the steering-wheel instead of in the floor, or perhaps it was the other way round, but Feredun was jubilant. He had been slaving at an extra part-time job to get the money for this car so I strove to be genuinely impressed, despite not knowing what a 'clutch' was in English let alone German or Persian. He just grinned and was eager to show off the car by taking me to Karadj, and there was nothing I wanted more just then than some lonely countryside and Yorkshire-like snow. I had been dreaming of Blake Dean and the winter heron in a vain search for food.

The snow in some of the northern side-roads lay still untouched, but as we neared the highway the car hissed through black water while the uncompleted blocks of flats being built there rose like salt caves on each side. The workers in baggy Turkish trousers and brown and white woollen hats live on the sites, and I had been fascinated from the first time I saw it how on arrival at the site they build a temporary but perfect house of loose bricks for themselves. Later, when the horizontal and cross supports of the main building are erected, but without the walls, they live inside the frame. After the building workers, came the unbroken white of snow-covered desert at the foot of the mountains.

I breathed a sigh of relief—Teheran and its problems seemed to have vanished.

Feredun was still in raptures about his car; he chose this moment to reveal a small refrigerator where in summer bottles of beer could be kept cool. Now it held some sandwiches and a bottle of white wine.

'We'll stop at the dam,' he said. 'Even if it's below freezing outside, the air-conditioning's so good in here we don't really need clothes.'

I uh-huhhed thoughtfully, and cast a look at the nearest mountain to see if I could spot the dazzle of a telescope trained on us by the ever-efficient police. All I saw, however, was a large bird, but I refrained from asking Feredun to identify it as natural history did not inspire him.

'The seats go back. We could sleep all night in this car,' he said happily.

We drove on towards the dam. The thinnest reeds had become thick glass rhubarb-stalks, and the water in the shallows was skinned with pale ice. The wintry stretch of water looked immense and empty.

As we ate the sandwiches and drank the wine from paper-cups, I said casually, 'Feredun, the Goethe Institute is offering scholarships for studying in Germany.'

'The authorities here wouldn't like it. You know so many Iranian doctors stay in Germany and America.'

'But they're coming back now,' I pointed out. 'You could go easily, especially if you undertook to serve afterwards in this country for five years.'

'In some shitty little village near the Pakistan border!'

'That would be true service, more than being a court physician and attending to the Shah's piles. And even that is more use than being dead.'

In the long silence he smoked a cigarette.

'You think I should go?' he said at last in a small voice.

I handed him the forms from the Goethe Institute. 'The closing date is the end of this week.'

'I'll think about it. They mightn't take me.'

Clouds took the sun. The whiteness held a menacing gloom.
Reversing the car on the ice was not easy. Silently we headed
back to the city. I had destroyed, for that day, his delight in the
car.

I spent Christmas Day alone in the house. I had again
wedged foam-rubber into the buzzer and did not have the
telephone plugged in. Feredun had his keys if he wished to see
me, but he did not come. He might have been working as
Christmas Day, falling on a Thursday, was no different from
others in a Muslim country.

The snow fell, mounting in the little garden beyond the
reed-blinds, and the sky was so dark that even in the daytime
the light had to stay on.

I had a feeling that anything might happen—soldiers sur-
rounding the house, or Esmail sending Kamal with a message
that Feredun could not go off to Germany just when he pleased.
I even feared that they might kill him.

My head ached and I was certain of nothing. I had planted
some seeds in plant-pots and in the silent room I seemed to
hear them invisibly stirring and the snowflakes whispering in
secret acitivity. I was full of dread as if an explosion were in
train and in the meantime I could not bear the false-alarms
of the buzzer.

It was New Year's Eve before Feredun appeared, with a
black eye, an arm in a sling and a painful limp. As there was
a taxi-driver carrying a load of cases behind him, I could not
voice all my alarms immediately. Fortunately the ladies above
were not at home, to come down and make a clamour about
the injured Feredun, as they had gone off to buy a sheep for an
approaching religious festival.

Feredun was somewhat truculent, demanding to know where
I had been, as the hospital had tried repeatedly and in vain
to contact me by telephone.

'Hospital?' I gaped weakly.

He began to tell me about the blood-transfusion, only pausing
parenthetically to ask what there was to eat, and the blood-
transfusion became mixed in my mind with the sheep that
would before long have its throat cut before my windows. I

had some German bacon and a Christmas pudding in the refrigerator—neither seemed quite suitable for a Muslim friend. But Feredun claimed that he could not walk a few streets to a small Iranian restaurant so I set the Christmas pudding boiling—a long process—and he filled in the interval with bacon and eggs.

'Did they attack you?' at last I managed to ask.

Feredun looked at me in amazement, and said irritably, 'The policemen got his name. I couldn't move my arm, or I would have walloped him.'

'Who?'

'The other driver so-called. Son of a dog! They don't know how to drive in this country. They bash along like anarchists.'

'You mean you were in an accident?'

'Do I look as if I've been having my photograph taken?'

I was amazed. 'But what about Esmail and Kamal? How did they take it about applying for a scholarship?'

'What could they say? They weren't too pleased about the accident, but they weren't brought into it. The car's a complete write-off.'

So nothing had been as I imagined and expected.

Suddenly I had the problem of feeding a Feredun who grumbled if he had to limp a few streets to a nearby restaurant and liked to have an hour-long piping hot shower when no household geyser in Iran held such an amount of water. He was endlessly on the phone wrangling with the insurance company and going off, with much grumbling, to pressure the other driver who was, apparently, counter-suing.

However, as his blood-transfusion settled down and his bruises began to blend in, I was pleased on coming back from work to find that he had prepared an Iranian salad and tidied up the place. As liniment took the strains out of his arm and leg he regained his old vigour and in the mooncold January nights we would go together to small Armenian restaurants.

He was friendly with everyone; his face was full of laughter and so people responded warmly to him. He used to chat with the man in the local flower shop and was offered roses at a discount. As a result our house was never without a bowl of roses, that held their freshness as they uncinctured their petals

in the cold weather. In my mind I tried to make the days un-
fold as slowly as the winter roses, to retard the sweet time, for
each day was bringing nearer his departure.

Yet he had to go, the sooner the better. I dreaded the arrival
of his air-ticket, but till it did come, I feared that the secret
police might break in on us to carry him off.

One morning I found him crying into the pillow. In the end
I asked, awkwardly, what was the matter.

'Kamal, Nasir. I won't see them again.'

'We're together.'

'In Germany I won't see you either.'

'It's not so far,' I said. 'In the summer I could take buses
to München across Turkey.'

I did not know if he suspected, or even knew, that Esmail
was about to do something that would have serious con-
sequences, of if he were grieving at the separation from a
group of friends that had been like a family for him. And
Germany? I did not really know that I would be there. My
head felt like exploding. But if he did not get right away from
the danger, the explosion would be real from guns in the yard
of a military barracks.

CHAPTER SIX

At last the time came to depart. The Lufthansa plane left at seven in the morning, and this meant he would have to be at the airport at five. Accordingly we scarcely slept at all, from worry, that we would not wake up in time.

The evening before he had packed, with irritating perfection, and afterwards became sombre.

'What's the matter?' I asked.

He sighed gloomily. 'I don't think I'll like Germany.'

'But you've been there,' I pointed out. 'You loved it.'

'I didn't like the toilets,' he said.

'Toilets? What's the matter with German toilets?'

'I don't like the paper,' he said seriously. 'A Persian toilet is so much nicer with the water. One feels fresher.'

'Heavens,' I said, 'there's no problem. All you've got to do is take an ewer with you and fill it up with water whenever you go into a lavatory. There's no shortage of water in Western Germany.'

'It's an idea. But I haven't got an ewer.'

'Take the one here.'

'It's not new and clean.'

'I'll go and buy you one,' I said. 'They cost very little.'

'Do you think the German Customs will make objections?'

'Of course not. If they look, they may want to know what it's for. Tell them it's a milk jug as you have to drink goat's milk,' I improvised.

We had to stuff his slippers and soap into the ewer before we could pack it into the case.

At the airport the Iranian party, for West Germany, was already assembled and Feredun was swept with them into the departure lounge. From the tarmac, big and strong and smiling he waved to me, and at last the plane rose up taking him out of sight into the future. He was safe.

The telephone did not ring. The outside buzzer was pressed only by *naft* men or beggars. The paraffin space-heater puffed and panted, and the snowflakes slid silently outside. I might have been living on a tundra instead of in the centre of a city; the snow muffled all.

In the room I had the snow of thousands of examination papers, on subjects that I would not have inflicted on Adolf Hitler let alone on innocent eager young minds, and when these had me demented I played Mozart and Schubert on cassettes to let in a ray of sanity. I wished almost I had never known Feredun if I had to suffer now this absence of human companionship, but then I wondered what loneliness he was enduring. But among German students he would be devouring sausages in all sorts of dives. No German city surely could be as inhospitable as Teheran.

One evening when rain had earlier washed away most of the snow and the sky was clear, I decided to break out of the boredom of marking papers and indoors existence by going to a restaurant, not one of the small local places, but a French or Russian one. Not many taxis were running so I walked along Fisherabad to the Ferdousi Circle. Caviar and cream seemed too rich, so I had a French meal, an exquisitely cooked fish.

After the tip, I had just fifteen rials left, enough for a *jitney*-taxi back if I caught one at the corner of Pahlavi Avenue. I passed the Shah Reza police-station and the hotel. At the corner of Pahlavi I could see a group of people, but the intersection was usually busy with many people waiting there for taxis.

The sky was clear with stars; the jubes ran swift and high with melting snow. The trees seemed to be breathing a deep peace. I had not been out alone in Teheran at night for so long that I had forgotten the original reason for caution. As I stepped into the roadway to call my destination to an orange-taxi, a half-brick came down on my skull and a knife went into my side.

There was no policeman on one of the opposite corners, and he would have probably have got out of sight quickly. A crowd of late-night drinkers from a vodka-shop watched with the faint curiosity of Iranians on such occasions; no one **comes** forward to help. In the street-lighting I saw the faces of my attackers clearly—the one (with the half-brick) was a young rather feminine-faced fellow, but the other with the knife had a screwed-up monkeyish face and a kind of demented energy as he dragged me forward and drove the knife in repeatedly. I could have—my mind worked the possibilities clearly—given him a blow to the throat or neck, but if my concentrated strength had killed him before witnesses then I would have been held guilty of his murder despite the provocation given me, and the knife could have plunged into my heart or one of my eyes. By now they had me in the darkness of a side-road, where there was an uncompleted building, into the basement of which we rolled. The younger one had grabbed at my pockets and taken out a crumpled packet of cigarettes, holding five Winstons. The motive for the attack was thus revealed as robbery, though monkey-face had a blood-lust as he gripped me and slashed. The younger one had ripped the belt from my trousers and one of my shoes had come off. I fell backwards into a pit. Above they struck matches. I heard the younger one bleating in fear about police. The other threw earth and stones down at me; I heard the scrabble of departing feet, and then in echoing vaulted emptiness the rumble of a metal gate.

I removed the dry foundation-soil from my face, shook the earth and stones from my body and in the darkness clambered upwards. There was total darkness and silence in the foundations of the incompleted building. I crawled upwards and after what seemed hours bumped into what seemed to be a wall. There was nothing to indicate direction and I hoped it was not an inner dividing wall. I followed it along to the left and was finally rewarded by seeing a faint light from the street. Before me was a wire-mesh grating used for garage doors. I hoped they had not locked it from the outside. But when I pushed it squeaked and rumbled upwards, and I sprawled into the side-street.

I was almost naked as my clothes had been sliced into strips and my face and body were dripping with blood. One shoe was no use so I left it there and walked into Pahlavi Avenue. The taxis did not stop, then a private taxi-driver with a friend sitting beside him stopped and offered to take me for a hundred rials. I waved him on. Then a private car stopped—the driver laughed at my appearance, not unkindly, and said he would take me home.

'Fifteen rials,' I said for the small sum of money had been in my hand all the time. He waved the money aside, so I got in beside him. He handed me a box of paper tissues, and I began to wipe the blood from my eyes and face.

'Do you want the police?' he asked.

'God no,' I said. The thought of the bureaucracy—and monkey-face was such a psychopath he would strike again, in less favourable circumstances, and soon enough be in prison —again, as his dehumanized behaviour suggested to me that he had just come out of an institution. The south of the city had terrible deprivation when people would kill for five cigarettes and a cheap belt.

I thanked my rescuer, and though it was late I ran the shower and washed all the blood from me and stuck band-aids over the cuts. Only now I realized my left hand was broken, but I was lucky the knife had not gone into a vein. I had a meeting in the morning. If I combed my hair down, the wound in my head would not be visible, and I would try to buy some penicillin-ointment to keep the cuts from becoming septic.

I took some passion-flower tablets to ensure a deep sleep, as my hand and body ached, and slept soundly.

CHAPTER SEVEN

In the early summer, when I was going about the airline com-
panies trying to find the lowest prices to Europe, I was tempted
by an apple-pie in a shop window. Inside the shop I noticed
that there was a tea or coffee shop in the back, and I was going
in when a young woman greeted me and smilingly motioned
me to sit down at her table.

I could not place her at once. Then: 'You're Kamal's sister,'
I recognized. The shy schoolgirl of that remote morning was
hard to identify in this much older-looking girl. I asked con-
ventionally how they all were.

She dropped her head. 'He's in prison.' She spoke very softly.
'My mother and father are broken. They're allowed to see him,
though.'

'What happened?' A man came and I ordered tea.

'It wasn't in the papers. They held up a bank to get money
for arms from Iraq. Nasir and Esmail Karim-zadeh were
condemned to death and shot. He was jailed for three years.'

'He was lucky,' I said dully, realizing that he must have
co-operated and so betrayed the others to have received such a
comparatively light sentence. But I was seeing Nasir's quiet
far-away look and had the smell of his skin in my nostrils. I sat
numb.

'He's not.' She was almost crying. 'He can be tried over and
over again for the same thing. And a life-sentence is a sentence
for life here.'

I remembered his saying, 'We can die for it,' but it was the
other two who had died. For nothing; not even publicity for
their motives had been allowed.

'You're upset.' There was a touch of satisfaction in her voice.

'I didn't know. I'm sorry for you and your family. It was so
pointless.'

But I had got Feredun off in time, I thought; he must have

known, or was it a piece of madness they had brewed up later?
Romantic amateurs.

I paid the bill and saw her to a taxi. I was going in the same
direction but I did not take the taxi with her. I needed to walk
in the sunshine under the still young leaves.

The façades and windows of the banks and government
buildings gleamed opulently, dead materials. O Nasir, your
body is gone forever.

Portraits of the Shah were in every window.

Patience. Craft.